PARADISE OF THE WOLF

BENJAMIN J. BURTON

• Chicago •

PARADISE OF THE WOLF

BENJAMIN J. BURTON

Published by
Joshua Tree Publishing
JoshuaTreePublishing.com
• Chicago •

13-Digit Print ISBN: 978-1-956823-44-8

Front Cover Credit: Miami Skyline, Michael Adobe Stock
Front Cover Credit: Wolf, TRAVELARIUM Adobe Stock
Back Cover Credit: Santeria, Kia Adobe Stock

Disclaimer:
This is a work of fiction. Names, characters, places, and incidents are the product of the author's imagination or have been used fictitiously. Any resemblance to actual persons, living or dead, events, locales or organizations is entirely coincidental.

Printed in the United States of America

DEDICATION

I would like to thank everyone whose input and confidence in me have made this work possible. Thanks to the support of my family, friends, and colleagues. I'd also like to thank my good friend Krystal Watts for her patience with all the late nights and early mornings, without which I wouldn't have had the motivation or energy to push on through.

Special thanks go out to Justin Fodo and James Holifield for their help with proof reading.

Finally, a big thanks to my Mother for pushing me along when I lost sight of my vision by teaching me to never let other tell me the limits of my capability.

Enjoy!

"One day you'll wake up and there won't be any more time to do the things you've always wanted. Do it now."
— Paulo Coelho

Prologue

The fight between good and evil exists. These are not just abstract concepts. These are the maps in which we navigate life.

When the world is burning down around us, then that is when we can understand what it means to be on both sides of this war. It is in those moments that our choices become clear. If you do nothing, then you have chosen evil; if you act on behalf of justice, then you have chosen good.

I believe the same is true for all of us. When we see someone struggling with their own self-doubt, we must call them out. We must show them how they can overcome anything that stands in their way. When we see someone being bullied, we must stand up and protect them, even if they are someone who does not deserve it. That is the nature of good people: we all want everyone to be able to live their life with dignity, even those who don't deserve it. I know that most of us will never go through a situation where we must make such decisions, but as someone who has many times, I find comfort in knowing that when I did, my mind was clear enough to know exactly which side I should choose.

And so, I say to you now: Choose. Choose to be a hero, choose to believe in the light. Choose to believe in good over evil. Choose to put others before yourself. And choose to spread the word of what it means to be a hero.

Benjamin J. Burton

THE BEAST

For me, it is not hard to understand. At my core, I am like all of you. I have a WONDERFUL, BEAUTIFUL NEED. I am compelled to misbehave sometimes to fulfill that need!

I cannot fight The Hunger.

The Hunger always seems to win.

In the past, I tried my best to tamp down this presence, that other part of me that is always fighting for dominance, but later I found it much more enjoyable to let it out as much as possible.

My playtime would not be denied.

What I see daily amazes me as I walk among you—eating at your restaurants and cafes and sitting at your parks and gardens. Walking among you on your streets, and you, oblivious to me.

Oblivious to death.

You have such pitifully short lifespans; yet, you insist on constantly undertaking dangerous pastimes that put you quickly in my path. You are all so fragile, your lives so finite, yet most of you do little with your insignificant existence.

As I said before, I used to fight it. I thought myself the captain of this vessel of flesh and blood, but now, I don't know how I would live without it, how I could EVER live without that, THRILL! The thrill of the hunt. The smell of sweat and blood, of life's essence! Hearing of my prey's rapid breathing in their attempt to cling to life a little longer. The scent of all that FEARRRR!!

At times the chase is almost more fulfilling than what I get to their end. That fresh taste of blood. That look in your eyes. When I see you make the realization that what you knew as life is OVER—AND THERE WAS NOTHING YOU CAN DO ABOUT IT!

I don't feel bad for you. You CHOSE long ago to abandon that primal part of your brain that can sense that something is wrong in the universe, that something is in error, that the Spector of Death is infiltrating your ranks! Ages ago, humankind listened to that instinct, that voice. There was an acceptance, an unwritten covenant, that there are powers in this world that are beyond explanation or comprehension! In an age of science and technology, arrogance, comfort, and disbelief of the old ways have issued you a false sense of security. Yet despite all you think you have accomplished, you are still the best of my playtime friends!!

This will be an excellent year, and I look forward to our great game.

I wish you the best of luck.

Regards,
The Beast

CHAPTER 1

HOMESTEAD, FLORIDA: 2 PM EST

This heat is fucking insane, Louisa thought.

Homestead was about two to three hours north of Key West. Growing up in South Florida, you would have thought she would be used to it, but the heat became more unbearable every year. If Louisa had the money, she thought, she would move near her cousin in upstate New York to feel what real winter was like, with snowstorms and all. Who knows, maybe she would like it so much she would never leave!

The car ride felt like a lifetime as she approached the town of Homestead. The city looked like any other small South Florida city—the buildings were cookie-cutter houses that seemed to go on for miles and miles. At this point, the city's outskirts were starting to give way to sprawling farmland. She could see several barns along the roadside, and rows of crops were growing between each farm. There weren't many cars passing by either; dawn was hours away, and she still had two to three hours before she made it home.

Ugh! I can't wait to get out of this car! Louisa thought angrily after another hour of driving. *I'm going to need a drink when I get there.*

She rolled down her window and let the hot air blow through the car. Maybe that would help cool her off? She was sure it wouldn't make much difference, but anything was better than sitting here. She glanced at her phone and saw it was 2 a.m.

"Shit," she cursed under her breath, "my parents are probably already asleep."

She turned on the radio and tried to stay awake by listening to the news station. She hoped they had something interesting to report so she could pass the time. But no such luck. They just repeatedly talked about the same things: the weather, traffic accidents, murders . . . Nothing exciting was going on in Miami. At least not for now.

Suddenly, her car stopped running. It was a miracle that she managed to get off the Ronald Reagan Turnpike before the car died. She would have been urged to get on what passed for a shoulder if it broke there. The Ronald Reagan Turnpike traveled through eleven counties in Florida. Fast drivers, road debris, and vacationers made this interstate somewhat treacherous to travel.

With cars going between fifty and one hundred miles an hour at 2 a.m., she managed to get the car to a much better location by sheer luck. To add to her misfortune, since the car died, the AC also died, no longer shielding her from the brutal Florida summer. Even at 2 a.m., it had to be at least 90 degrees out there. She was lucky enough to find a small dirt road leading away from the highway. Being a smart girl, she knew that once she got off the road, she should probably stay there. There were plenty of places to hide. Louisa didn't know how long she would be stranded, but she knew that it wasn't safe to drive any further. After all, she was a woman alone, late at night, not far from where the drug dealers and pimps ruled the streets. Her mind began to wander as she sat in the car waiting for someone or something to come along—and hopefully help her out.

"Oh God," she whispered under her breath, "Please let me make it."

The thought of being raped or murdered crossed her mind again, and she tried to fight the fear with thoughts of freedom. She was so terrified that she could barely think straight. She tried to calm herself down, but the heat inside the car seemed to be increasing rapidly. The air coming through the open window just made things worse. As far as Louisa knew, this place was uninhabited, but she still felt like there might be people around somewhere. Maybe they passed by when she was driving and didn't see her? What if she ran into some kind of wild animal? They said alligators lived out here . . . and there were snakes too! She shuddered at the idea of having one of those slither up on her.

She pulled out her phone and checked for service, hoping she might have a signal. But there was nothing. No bars, no internet, nothing. Just silence. She looked outside. It wasn't a big area to begin with, and she could hardly see anything. She couldn't tell how close she was to the highway anymore.

I'm stuck here? Louisa thought. If somebody comes along and decides to rape me, no one will hear my screams over the traffic, and even if they did, who's going to help me? My momma raised me right, taught me how to defend myself. I'll kick his ass and run like hell! She couldn't remember exactly when she first started fantasizing about kicking some asshole's ass, but she sure loved it now. She remembered the first time she ever tried to fight back against a man trying to take advantage of her. A painful memory came to her.

As a teenager, she had been walking home from school late one day. She didn't live very far away, so she figured she should walk. That way, if she happened to get lost, it wouldn't be too far to get home. Little did she know that the one thing she should not have done was walk home. She hadn't gotten far when she felt a hand touch her butt. She quickly spun around, ready to give him a piece of her mind, only to see it was the local high school football star, Robby White.

His eyes lit up as he saw her, just as she expected. He smiled and said, "Hey baby, you want a ride?"

He walked closer to her. Louisa was close enough now that she could smell his cologne and feel his breath on the back of her neck. Her body began to tremble as she looked into his blue eyes and waited for him to speak.

"Well, are ya gonna say yes or am I gonna have to make ya bitch?"

His hands moved down to grab her breasts, squeezing them roughly. She resisted at first, then let go, letting her head fall forward. He leaned in, reaching for her mouth.

"If you don't kiss me, I'll take it as a 'no,'" he whispered.

Louisa quickly opened her mouth, feeling his tongue invade her mouth. She quickly pulled away and ran towards home. That was the first time, and only time that she ever fought back. Other times, though, she knew to just keep quiet. She learned to play the game but always kept one step ahead. Now, as she sat in a shitty car, late at night, waiting for a savior to show up, she wondered if she had been played. Was this some kind of test—or was it just chance that she was stuck out here? Either way, she was getting tired of being treated like a piece of meat.

She rolled down her window more, allowing more of the hot air to come inside, hoping it might cool things off a bit. It didn't work. Instead, it seemed to make the situation worse. Sweat dripped from her nose and chin. Her clothes clung to her skin, sticking to her flesh. She reached behind her head, untying her ponytail, letting it fall down her back. In the dark, she watched her reflection in the side mirror, seeing her long black hair swaying in the breeze. She turned, looking in the rearview, watching the back of her own head. She slid the keys from the ignition and brought them up to her lips. She kissed each of the key fobs, making sure she gave each one equal attention. Then, she put them back in the ignition and pulled out the plastic bottle of water she had bought earlier. She took another sip, letting it roll down her throat, washing the taste of stale beer from her mouth. She closed her eyes, resting her head back, listening to the crickets chirping.

She opened her eyes, feeling the sticky sweat run between her breasts and drip down her stomach. Her bra was soaked through. She wanted nothing more than to get out of the car, strip down, and lay on the grass beneath a tree, letting the sun dry her out. She tried not to think about how the heat would bake her body. How it would cook her like an egg in a pan. She focused instead on the night sky above, leaning against the steering wheel, closing her eyes again. She let herself go, falling back into the darkness, allowing the world to spin away from her.

Her eyes flew open again. She sat upright, looking at the road directly in front of her. The road was empty. She glanced back and forth, hoping that she wasn't imagining things. Still nothing. The sun had set hours ago; there was no chance that anyone would be out this late. She sighed, rolling up the window.

When she had stopped for gas a few hours ago on the way back from Jacksonville to see some old friends, she thought she would have enough cigarettes to last until she got home. She did not anticipate that she would end up in the middle of nowhere with three cigs left.

Fuck my life, she thought.

To add to her discomfort, the street she was forced to stop on was barely lit, in the middle of a ghost town, if you could even call Homestead a town. She called her useless boyfriend three times; all the calls went to voice mail. He was probably flirting, or maybe screwing that damn bartender he was ogling at the Aqua Bar, thinking she missed him undressing the bartender with his eyes. When she started dating him, at least to Louisa, it was evident that he was far from marriage material. Still, Key West was a small community. Everybody knew everybody, and none of the other guys who approached her at the time held her interest.

Louisa was not vain, but she knew the effect she had on the opposite sex. She was about average height, had long black hair, and decent T and A if she said so herself. She had been told that she had an athletic body, though she couldn't remember the last time she stepped into a gym. She also was told she had a great tan, given to her care of the great Southern Florida weather, which, while she enjoyed most of her time on the beach, she was not enjoying very much right now. Her present predicament made her think about how people took luxuries like artificially cooled air for granted all the time! She decided to smoke another cigarette, hoping it would cool her off a bit, as well as give her something to do rather than sit here and wait for someone to come along and steal her car.

She could imagine the headlines: "Local woman loses car and turns up missing, the only thing found of her remains were empty packs of cigarettes."

Louisa thought of herself as a tough girl although there were more brutal places to grow up than Key West. Growing up with three brothers, however, would make any girl tough. She was not the type to jump at any real or imagined sight or sound like in those cheesy movies, but this place gave her the creeps. While she didn't like the prospect of leaving her boyfriend's car abandoned here in the middle of nowhere, the bastard was not answering his phone. She hoped the rendezvous with that slut at the Aqua Bar was worth it.

Homestead, Florida, was known for its high crime rate, and he might find his car on blocks tomorrow before the tow truck made it here. She hated this car. Louisa personally thought the car wasn't worth the effort of stealing, but she didn't have her car, so she was in no position to judge. An old 1989 Camaro, with the paint peeling off of what was once a pristine red paint scheme, now looked like an ugly, depressing orange. The orange hue symmetrically matched the rust patches accumulated over time on various locations of the car's body. The interior wasn't much better; holes and cigarette burns littered the leather upholstery and dash of the vehicle.

It would take, like . . . a week of shampooing and uninterrupted vacuuming to get the smoke smell out of this piece of shit, Louisa thought. To top it all off, he actually had a pair of fuzzy dice hanging from the mirror! They were his lucky dice, or so he claimed. He said they helped him win at the races. She could only assume that they did nothing but make him look more pathetic than he already was. That shit was soooo played out. What a cliche!

She was going to light one of the three crumpled cigarettes she had left when she saw something that made her pause. Was it her imagination, or could she see what looked like yellow or gold pins of light through an unkempt group of tall grass, bushes, and palm trees on her left, off the shoulder of the road? She threw away the cigarette, then put her windows up, only to realize how ridiculous the action was.

If somebody, or something, wanted in this car enough, they, or it, would find a way to get in.

She was getting so nervous that she was starting to forget about the uncomfortable heat in the car. She needed to get out of here! Get out of this spooky ass town. She was beginning to get scared.

She started going through her phone to find the app for Uber. She seriously wondered if there was a fleet of cars driving people around Homestead at this hour, but it was her best option. She could always try one of her friends, but she didn't want to be inconvenient. If waiting for the Uber ended up being a long wait, which the app would show, then she would go that route. She was just about to activate the app to get a driver when the dots started . . . moving.

She tried to open the app; she wasn't getting any service!! She was changing phone providers at the first opportunity!

"Fuck it," Louisa said. If someone were getting woken up tonight, she would apologize to them later! She looked up her friend Lisa's number; Lisa was her ride-or-die, and she hardly ever let her down. When Louisa explained the situation and conveyed the mounting dread she was starting to feel, Lisa would understand and forgive her. Once she answered the damn phone!

The dots were moving to her left. She wasn't sure, but she thought she could see the vegetation surrounding the dots being disrupted. Like something was moving through it!

What in God's name made her decide to stop on the only road in Florida with . . . no . . . fucckkking . . . lightsss! she thought.

She was sweating more profusely now, and not because of the heat.

Lisa's phone kept ringing, and ringing, ringing, and ringing.

Ringing and ringing.

The dots abruptly changed direction, going to the right.

The dots seemed to be . . . what, playing with her? she thought with some confusion.

"This is Lisa; I'm not available at this time; please leave a message," squawked Lisa's voicemail.

The dots disappeared.

Louisa exhaled loudly; she didn't realize that she had been holding her breath the whole time.

"Holy shit!" she screamed as the dots moved into the undergrowth, and out of sight. She had no idea what they were at this point, probably some kind of wildlife. But there was definitely an unnatural aspect to it all that was bothering her. And now she felt like someone, or something, was watching her from behind the thick canopy of trees. The sound of leaves rustling on the ground next to her started her heart racing even more, but then stopped when she realized it was a squirrel scurrying away from her.

"Oh my God! Squirrels," she said in a tiny voice, trying not to scare it off. "I'm going crazy."

She chuckled at herself nervously and sat back down on the seat.

Was she seeing things?

She tried to redial her shit-bag boyfriend, but it went to voicemail . . . again.

Louisa thought about walking to the next available gas station. She changed her mind for two reasons.

The first reason was she felt ridiculous just walking into the night in some random direction with a little or unknown destination. Though the prospect of finding an area with better reception sounded very appealing, she needed to figure out how far she would have to walk. It could be sunrise by the time she found a place with good bandwidth or a person that could lend her a phone. That option was off the table.

The second reason was that she doubted whether that was even necessary. She thought she could eventually find a phone number to dial for an Uber, but she didn't know a number to dial. And, with her lack of Wi-Fi reception, she couldn't look for one on the internet.

I could just walk a few paces away from the car and see if my reception improves, Louisa thought.

That was when the driver's side window shattered, and a razored-edged, fur-covered claw gauged a chunk of meat from Louisa's left shoulder. Blood streaked all over the inside of the shitty car.

Louisa put her hands up in defense and waited for the inevitable outcome, and. . . . nothing!

She had to make a run for it. Louisa flung herself over to the passenger side. Despite her disorientation and blood loss, she was conscious that she wasn't being attacked by . . . whatever that was!

Then . . . the car suddenly started rocking violently!

What she saw in her rearview mirror defied comprehension.

She saw those same two yellow, golden dots, but now she could see a little of what they were attached to. Whatever it was, it was HUGE! Despite the limited visibility, the full moon was out; she could see the profile. The creature seemed about six or seven feet tall. She only saw its silhouette. It looked human in shape but covered with . . . fur that appeared to gleam red in the moonlight!

She wanted to open the door and run . . . anywhere, but she was paralyzed with fear! She knew she had to go for it, or she would die here! The end of the street in front of her looked more well-lit than where she was present. If she made a run for it . . . maybe someone could help her! She needed someone to help her!

She bolted out of the passenger side. The creature grabbed her leg and pulled her back against the car. It then ripped into her with its razor claws and tore off her left arm, leaving behind a bloody stump. It continued to rip until she stopped moving.

By the time the car's shaking had come to a halt, Louisa was dead.

When the homeless man known as Jedd the Drunk was interviewed later by the police, he told them that he could recall the screams, which seemed to go on for a long time, then subside into liquid gurgles, like someone drowning. He also said he heard what he thought were sounds of snapping bones and squishy eating sounds, like the sound a dog would make if you gave it a good bone. To his mind, they were in no way human-sounding. Then came a silence so deep that even the sound of his own heart beating seemed loud. And all at once, the sounds stopped. The silence lasted a very long time. Then there was another scream or cry or moan—this one more desperate than any of the others Jedd had heard. This continued until finally it tapered off into a final gasp and nothing more. It was over.

What he didn't tell the police, because they would probably think he was crazier than he thought he was, was a sound he had never heard before and would likely not stop hearing until the end of his days.

What . . . he thought . . . he heard was . . . a deep, guttural . . . laughter!

He would remember the laughter for the rest of his life.

Jedd's testimony was widely reported in the news, and every reporter and cop who covered the story became convinced that he was either crazy, or possibly telling the truth. A few cops thought he might be trying to cover up what he had seen because he was afraid people would think he was crazy. After all, this guy was homeless, and he drank heavily, so everyone thought it was odd that he would come forward to testify.

But Jedd didn't care about being thought of as crazy. He just wanted to be left alone. He knew they wouldn't believe him anyway, no matter how hard he tried to convince them. Years later, he would still wake up in the middle of the night with a terrible sense of foreboding, wondering if maybe it really happened after all.

The police did not believe him, nor the reporters. They had no idea what sort of animal could do what he claimed it did, and neither did any other law enforcement official from anywhere else in the world. He was just a crazy old man who had a few too many drinks on the beach that day.

The only thing everyone really agreed on was that something bad had happened to the woman. There was no doubt in their minds that she was dead.

But who killed her? And how? The police would never know. If she died under mysterious circumstances, that meant only one thing. It was murder, but there were no suspects or witnesses. No proof of anything. Nothing at all.

After several weeks of investigation, and an extensive search for the woman's remains, Louisa's body was never found.

CHAPTER 2

HOMESTEAD, FLORIDA WEEKS EARLIER

Chelsi had the same nightmare again and again. She was running through what she thought was a forest. She could smell everything. She could smell the elm and ash trees. She could smell the grass and wildflowers; she could even smell the fog that had engulfed the night in an unearthly blue-gray hue illuminated by a bright blue moon.

She could also smell the blood, though she didn't know where it was coming from.

She could hear everything in the forest. Amorous foxes, rutting deer, screeching owls, and even hungry hedgehogs added to a cacophony of nighttime sounds. The moon and trees cast ominous shadows, while the sound of her footsteps crunching over twigs only added to her sense of isolation.

She could hear the old village bell ringing in the distance. She didn't know how she knew it was the village bell, which was ringing only to warn of approaching danger, but she knew.

Then all sounds in the forest ceased, except the cold and rustling leaves.

Her other sense, which only came to her at certain times of great peril, felt a presence. She could feel . . . IT!

She could see it in her mind. Feel its anticipation, excitement for a hunt, and she could feel its . . . hunger!

She could feel its golden eyes upon her, waiting to see what she would do. Would she run or face fate?

"Run!" the voice screamed in her head. "RUN! RUN NOW!"

She looked around for some place to hide, but there was nothing.

Tears rolled down her cheeks, she began running as fast as her feet would carry her!

* * *

Chelsi Villanueva woke up with a start, covered with sweat. Despite the hot South Florida temperature, she felt chilled to the bone. The alarm on her phone was shrieking incessantly to the point she thought it would explode in her hand when she picked it up. She looked at the time on the phone, and it was 6:30 a.m. She was going to be late again!!

Chelsi had woken up late like this for the third time this week; she felt exhausted and was dragging ass again! The nightmares were increasing in frequency and intensity! She thought that if they continued at this rate, she might have to seek a therapist or something. She'd never been one for therapy, but her dreams were getting really intense lately. She'd wake up feeling anxious and disoriented.

After she got out of bed, she dragged herself into the bathroom to take a shower. She took off her clothes and stood under the warm spray of the showerhead. It wasn't long before she was sobbing uncontrollably. Her sobs became louder and more desperate as her tears started flowing freely.

She pulled her hair back and squeezed some shampoo onto her hands. She made sure to get all of her body clean, including her scalp. Once she was done, she stepped out and dried herself off with a towel.

Once she had gotten dressed, she went downstairs and sat at the kitchen table with her breakfast. Chelsi was trying hard not to think about the dream or how bad she felt. The last thing she wanted to do was dwell on it. Instead, she focused on her morning routine in order to distract herself from dwelling on it, it didn't work. As soon as she finished eating, she went upstairs to get ready for her day. It was only 7:15 a.m. and she needed to leave by 8:00 a.m. if she was going to make it to work on time.

"Damnit!" she cursed to herself, "I'm always running late."

Chelsi threw her phone and keys on the counter and began to apply her makeup. Her eyes were puffy and red, but she knew she wouldn't be able to conceal them well enough. She didn't even try. Instead, she focused on highlighting her features to draw attention away from her tired eyes.

She brushed her teeth, put on deodorant, then applied her lipstick. Once she was done, she grabbed her bag and headed downstairs.

Miami traffic at 7 a.m. is brutal. Chelsi knew this for a fact because she had grown up with it. She was a born and bred Miamian, or whatever people not from Miami called people from Miami. She didn't remember the morning commute being like this when she was younger. The roads were jammed to the brim as cars and busses tried to get through the city. It took her thirty minutes just to drive two miles to work. Usually, she would wake, shower, drink coffee, get ready, and be on the road at least 30 minutes before the morning traffic hit the roadways, Turnpike, and freeways that made Miami and South Florida.

Chelsi loved Miami. There was always something to do, and the weather was great. On days like these, however, she seriously considered moving to some Podunk town upstate near Canada, with a population of less than 2000 and only two streetlights in the whole town!

Chelsi resigned herself to the realization that it would be a long day. It was getting close to the holiday season, so everyone smart had already put in their leave. Though it was known to get as hot as Florida elsewhere in America, there were days when it would reach the temperature of 80 to 90 degrees, even in January! Most of her coworkers would be home or out of town for Father's Day and Juneteenth, while Chelsi would sit in front of a computer screen for a twelve-hour shift with hardly any calls, though the overtime would be good, and she didn't have a life anyway.

The workdays were riddled with dull, cloying boredom, but sometimes, a little quiet boredom was not such a bad thing. Chelsi scooped up her keys, did a last check to ensure she remembered everything, then headed out the door. Her mind could wander, and occasionally it would take her back to another place and time.

Chelsi took a deep breath, leaned forward in her seat, and thought about how much she missed not being close to her family in Miami, though it was only an hour away, it felt farther. She had been gone for almost six years now; her mother passed away at the Miami Cancer Institute three years ago after a short battle with breast cancer. She had just turned fifty-seven. It still hurt to think about it, and even though she had only seen her mother twice in those last few months of her life, the pain would never really go away. She remembered her mother lying on her deathbed, looking tired, weak, and defeated. Chelsi was sitting next to her, holding her hand, and reading to her from one of her favorite books, "The Count of Monte Cristo." It wasn't until later that Chelsi realized that her mother had been crying silently throughout the entire novel. Chelsi felt a pang of guilt, but it quickly disappeared.

"Mom, I wish I could have been a better daughter to you," she said quietly.

Her mother smiled slightly and squeezed her daughter's hand, then fell asleep again. Chelsi knew her mother was dying, and she did everything she could to make sure she was comfortable. Chelsi spent the night by her side, sitting vigil with her mother.

At 6:00 a.m., she woke to the sound of her phone ringing. It was her father calling to say goodbye. He told her he loved her and that he wished he had more time to spend with her. Even as she cried, she felt her heart swell with love for him. His words were nothing like what she expected. Her father, who had always seemed so callous and selfish, was suddenly full of emotion. Now, she was stuck with a heartbroken man who refused to let his tears fall.

"I'm sorry, Dad," Chelsi said, wiping away the tears on her cheeks.

"It's okay, sweetie," he answered. "You've done your best. I know you are doing this for me."

"Daddy, what are you talking about, are you ok?" Chelsi asked, confused.

"I'm going to miss you so much," her dad said, his voice breaking with sorrow.

He had said it without any hint of sarcasm or malice. It was genuine sadness, and Chelsi wanted to cry all over again. "Don't worry, I'll come see you soon."

"Just promise me you won't stay away too long."

"I promise," he lied. That was two years ago.

She needed to collect herself and get her emotions under control. It was difficult because her father had always been so cold and distant. For most of her life, he had been absent, and only showed up every few months, usually just to argue with her mother. Their relationship had always been strained, but things got worse once she left. All of a sudden, he became very concerned with whether or not she was eating right, exercising enough, and how her grades were coming along. She wondered if he was genuinely worried about her health, or if he was just trying to feel important and needed. She knew he was probably the latter, but she did her best to appease him. After a while, she quit answering the phone, and started ignoring the texts. She was angry that he couldn't accept the way she lived her life, but she also felt guilty for abandoning him. Looking back, she realized that perhaps the fault belonged more with her than with her father. Perhaps if she had given him a bit more attention, he wouldn't have been so desperate to fill the void with her mother. Maybe she should have tried harder.

Chelsi's company was in Downtown Miami. Normally, she would take the Metrorail station near her house and then transfer to one of the express trains downtown. That meant she could be at work within ten minutes, but today she had no choice but to drive. Even if she went back home first, there wasn't enough time to make it to the station before they opened their doors at nine. So she drove all the way down Biscayne Boulevard into downtown. By the time she got off the highway, parked and made it inside, she felt like she'd run a marathon. Her boss was waiting for her at his desk with a smile on his face.

"Good morning," he said cheerfully. "I hear you're having car trouble."

"No, I'm fine," Chelsi replied. She sat down in front of him and immediately regretted her decision. She couldn't have been more tired if she tried.

"You look exhausted," he said and Chelsi knew that she did.

"Yeah, well, I've had a rough night." Chelsi rubbed her eyes trying to wake herself up. It didn't help.

* * *

CHAPTER 3

THE BEAST

I have been getting antsy these last couple of weeks. I need my "medicine." This oppressive heat was not helping.

"I miss the Old World," the Beast thought.

It was far easier to find playmates in the old days. You could catch someone walking through the forest by themselves at night. A poor fool walking home down a deserted street, thinking about the comforts of a home they will never see again! Some live alone or with others, all waiting for a savior or death. It was a more violent time, a beautiful, vibrant time. People came up missing daily. People were regularly beset by pestilence and famine in those gloomy days. They would expire at the hands of foul brigands and thieves. Often be put under the sword due to the frivolous conflicts and petty wars orchestrated due to the twisted and petty machinations of royals and nobles, who cared little for the people they claimed God appointed them to rule.

They would die due to sickness. The Great Plague took many souls in those dark days. It was *a great time of fun opportunities for me!! Oh! How the blood flowed in the good old days! I can still taste it!*

As the centuries trudged by, hunting started to become more complex. With their large cities and fortified homes, the meat brought a more remarkable skill in accounting for its population.

Humankind had also developed better tools to keep their families safe and the cold embrace of death at bay. They invented cannons that coughed fire like dragons of legend and could blow rocks asunder. Pistols and rifles that could strike you down with one blow! Now the meat have telephones with cameras owned by bored, nosey people. With all the machines, the smells and noise can be overwhelming sometimes! I see and feel it all. I see all of you cattle, your little lives and hopeless dreams—and the false safety you feel in your metal golems and concrete homes!

Fortunately for me, there was, and still is, opportunity for great fun!

The days of Old Jack are over. Though some beautiful monsters have followed his shining example since, and, at some times, surpassed him, though mailing a human kidney of one of his victims to the police had a certain ... flair to it!! Could the Ripper survive detection AND quench his appetites in the present day? I've seen this city change with my own eyes! There are new buildings now, many of them on fire. There are new streets too, but the old ones remain unchanged. The skyscrapers tower high above me, and the traffic roars about me like a herd of stampeding elephants.

But oh, how much quieter they would be if I were not here!

Cities can be so noisy. I understand why animals and birds flee from them. But, I love cities. I take pleasure in the noise and bustle. It's what makes it such an interesting place. A city is like a living animal in that respect. Cities are just so full of life!

I am certainly alive. I live in this city every night, and I know most of it like the back of my hand. I hear things I shouldn't hear, see things that should not be seen, and smell things no mortal should ever smell. That is one of the reasons why I have been able to endure for all these years. I've never been caught because I'm invisible.

Though, as I said before, the modern world is changing rapidly! Who knows where technology will lead us next!

The other reason I have survived so long is that I am careful. Very careful. I do not kill indiscriminately. I don't even eat children or anything easy to catch. I hunt the big game; I make myself scarce when people start to notice. People are so stupid. It's almost funny to watch them!

Then again, I suppose I was once one of those people, so I guess I cannot blame them entirely. People aren't very clever creatures. They're just too stupid and ignorant.

Don't get me wrong, I don't hate all of mankind. Some of you are good people, but it's hard to tell the difference between the good and the bad nowadays. Most of you are sheep. Sheep with guns who think they are wolves.

Still, I am a little surprised that I haven't been noticed yet. Even with all the changes in that have happened to this city over the years, I've been able to stay hidden. How long can this last? What happens when someone finally discovers me? Will I be discovered and killed, or will I find myself a nice, cozy cave somewhere and live out my days watching this city burn?

Only time will tell, but until then, I shall enjoy this city while I can.

Some things have stayed the same, like how I hunt my playmates! I find who I want to play the great game with. I follow them. Get them in my skin. You have to ask yourself, could one get to know their habits? Where do they work? How do they get work? Where do they go after work? What do they do in their homes where they think they are safe? Laughable!

You must always be disciplined and keep the hunger in check. That gets harder the closer you get to . . . playtime!

* * *

CHAPTER 4

HOMESTEAD, FLORIDA, THE MORNING OF LOUISA'S MURDER, 8:00 A.M.

John Abraham had been in law enforcement for almost 30 years, though it seemed to go by very fast! At one time, Homestead, Florida had the highest crime rate in Miami Dade County, so he thought he had seen it all. In an almost three decade career of gang shootings, drug overdoses, domestic violence, and missing person cases, he felt he had seen humanity at its lowest and most obscene state.

What he saw this morning forever changed his view of what the worst could be.

To say that there was blood everywhere was a gross understatement! Blood was on the street, the entire exterior, the front driver's side, and the passenger's side of the car. There was every indication that a grisly murder took place. The amount of blood was too much for anyone to survive losing and staying alive long. He had seen this bloody crime scene many times, but one glaring detail had him and everyone else at a loss.

There was no body present, only pieces of what once was part of a body! Flaps of skin and flesh decorated the entirety of the scene.

If it weren't for the registration located in the vehicle and the plates, they wouldn't have one piece of information to aid them in finding the identity of the "victim" or, an even more chilling scenario, "victims." The CSI folks were attacking the job of evidence collection with earnest.

The great importance of carrying out a murder scene investigation was to produce identification and evidence that can be used to disclose the cause of death and to obtain facts that can be used to bring the culprit to book in case of murder. Murder scene investigation involves a meeting place of law, logic, and science. Processing and handling the murder scene were very tedious and lengthy undertakings that required recognition, identification, documentation, collection of evidence, and analysis of the collected evidence. However, it also entailed careful examination and assessment of the crime site including its surroundings, the crime scene's environment, and the victim's body for any clues or sign that may relate to the crime itself, which, in this case, was proving to be difficult without a body.

The police had already contacted all hospitals in town but none of them reported any missing persons matching the description of the dead woman; nonetheless, they would continue their search until they found her.

Despite the initial difficulty finding the corpse and having no body to work with, the first thing on the agenda was to collect as much information about the deceased as possible—to collect the data relating to her life: who she was, where she lived, what she did for a living, and whom she interacted with before her disappearance. The next step was to reconstruct the time line of events related to the incident. As there was no body to examine, the detectives were forced to rely on circumstantial evidence. Based on this information, they could begin to theorize regarding the real cause of death.

First, they considered the possibility of foul play, then it turned into an accident, and finally, the hypothesis of suicide was raised after further analysis. In the end, however, they were unable to come up with a conclusive answer. It was unclear whether the woman committed suicide, or was murdered by someone else. There was no way of knowing for sure since she left no witnesses behind.

Usually, at this point, when they seal the entire area, law enforcers then move to the district attorney's chambers, where they obtain search warrants. This was important because, at times, some people could have prospects of privacy in portions of the murder scene. Also, the investigation process would be of little importance if not done legally since the findings wouldn't be admissible in court.

The issue was that there were NO leads at this time, or suspects to arrest and question!

They were not cutting corners, but they wanted to finish before the South Florida temperature started cooking everyone and everything in its vicinity. The medical examiner would likely have the report ready this evening. This with the backlog that had accumulated with murders in Miami, who knew when he would get the news? He didn't envy the medical examiner's job; he had his work cut out for him. DNA fingerprinting, also known as forensic DNA analysis, is the standard method law enforcers use to analyze evidence. This analysis is most reliable and affordable in such kinds of scenes. In connection to these, the analysis provides a faster identification mode once established settings like these. That old-ass Camaro probably had trace DNA dating back to when JOHN attended high school! Even if they pulled any DNA from the assailant, if the assailant had no record, their prints wouldn't turn up in the system, and John would be back to square one.

Whoever pulled this off was some freak of nature. To stalk someone, wait for the right opportunity to strike, then carry an entire body away without leaving any remains other than blood. There weren't any footprints in the blood. If there were, they had become obscured with various animals, birds, and insects that had curiously come to examine the remains that had once been Louisa Steinbeck, some for a potential meal to go. One thing was for sure; this wasn't this person or person's first time getting wet! He didn't believe that one person could stalk their victim, murder in a way that produced this much blood and have the strength to carry a whole body off in the night without causing a significant disruption and alerting everyone who lived close to the scene. As of now, he only had only one witness. He would have to get more information to make a conclusive theory. An unusual case, to say the least. He was trying to recall the details of the case, mainly as an exercise in procrastination. He did not want to make this next call to Louisa's parents. Informing loved ones of possible kidnappings or murders was always one of the worst parts of the job that hadn't become any easier in the last thirty years. John supposed it would be time to retire when it did become easier.

Everyone at the scene was so focused on not contaminating the crime scene by accidentally stepping in the blood and gore that they didn't find Louisa's left eyeball under the car until later that afternoon.

***

The Everglades, that evening

There are over 200,000 alligators living in the Everglades. Known by some to be the most enormous creatures in South Florida, reaching fourteen feet in length and weighing a thousand pounds, you could observe gators basking in the South Florida sun and heat, always keeping an eye open in anticipation of their next big catch. The Everglades was said to be the only place where alligators and crocodiles co-existed. It's unique because fresh water in Florida Bay meets the salt water of the Gulf of Mexico, creating a perfect ecosystem for both animals to live together. There are four alligator laws that every Floridian should know. One that it's illegal to feed alligators. Two, it is also illegal to kill wild alligators, and three, it is illegal to steal American alligator eggs. One more rule was paramount and usually went without saying.

It is illegal to feed human body parts to gators. But the Beast was never good at following the rules.

The Beast first attempted to dissolve the bodies with muriatic acid, but that didn't work well. Then lye, which didn't work fast enough. So the Beast had decided to try dumping the Playmates' remains into these alligator infested waters. That had worked out oh so much better!

The Beast thought that only someone mad would walk alone around these swamps at night. That made it the perfect place to take out the trash with total privacy and a lack of witnesses. Besides, the Beast knew that there were predators out there more dangerous than crocodiles and alligators! The reptiles made hissing sounds every time the Beast came here.

The Beast had made a point to study these fascinating creatures. Alligators and crocodiles were the closest to real dinosaurs left on earth. They had evolved into apex predators that have a solution for all their problems.

The alligator death roll is one such solution. Like crocodiles, alligators can't chew their food. They don't have molars, so they need to swallow their food whole.

The Beast started throwing the pieces of Louisa into the swamp.

The Beast remembered reading that it became more of a challenge when the animal was more significant than the alligator could swallow. So many alligators will use the death roll and slam their food onto rocks to break it down into smaller pieces.

As they smashed their food, which comprised of Louisa's arms, legs, and torso, they would swallow the smaller pieces that would start to break off the bigger sections. Then, if they struggled to get enough traction, they would wedge the piece of meat or kill between two rocks and use the death roll to take off parts, like a butcher chopping meat into smaller sections.

Alligators don't eat a large animal immediately, so they will use the death roll to break off parts as time passes. Alligators are not picky and will eat carrion; they are genuinely amazing creatures; it was always mesmerizing to the Beast to watch them do what they were created to do.

The Beast pulled out the last object from the jumble of plastic bags. They were always kept handy in the back of the well-kempt vehicle. Louisa Steinbeck's face peered back at the Beast with a frozen scream. The left side of her face was razored with incisions and gouges that went from her forehead down to her neck, making half her face unrecognizable. The facial muscle, insides of the sinus cavity, and portions of her orbital bones gleamed in the moonlight; the cuts went deep. Her left eye was missing already; what remained was a black hole giving an intimate glimpse into her orbital cavity. The other side of her face was much more recognizable; her dead, hazel eye stared at the Beast with such intensity that it was almost as if she was peering into Its soul. "If I even have a soul!" The Beast thought with amusement. The Beast started to caress the almost unblemished right side of Louisa's face. As it did, the hand enlarged and contorted to an inhuman size, the nails growing and turning black. Red fur was starting to grow on the back of the palm. The Beast's eyes gleamed with a mischievous golden yellow hue as It tossed the last of Louisa Steinbeck into the gator orgy of blood and meat.

If you ever asked anyone close the Chelsi Villanueva what kind of person she was, they would say that they thought of her as a practical, and down-to-earth person that could think through any situation or problem. They would say that she possessed an inner calm and accepted the highs and lows of her life with a compassionate and spiritual awareness. Men would say that Chelsi kept a curvaceous, hot, athletic figure with attractive body measurements and a beautifully shaped slim body type. When she was in high school, one boy even said she could pass for Eva Mendes on a good day.

She predictably had turned down his invitation to go out with him.The truth was that when she thought about it, they were both correct and not correct. She knew that didn't make much sense, but that was the best way she could explain it.

On some level, Chelsi knew that she was an attractive woman. Despite knowing this, she had and continued to struggle with issues pertaining to the opposite sex growing up. "Sometimes," Chelsi thought, "ignorance WAS bliss!"

Chelsi had secrets, secrets that only a few people were privy to. She can do . . . things, things that no other person she knew could do, maybe not everybody. Her Abuela, or grandmother, had gifts also. It was her mother's side of the family who were the receivers of the gifts and they passed them down to their children. Chelsi's mother didn't seem to know how to use them herself. When she'd seen some of what her daughter could do, she tried to stop it. That hadn't worked so well for her.

Her mother told her when she was a baby in the crib. Objects around her bedroom would rocket across tables and hit the walls. Sometimes these things would happen when Chelsi was asleep; sometimes, they would happen when she was awake; most of the time, they happened when she was irritable or angry, as babies are known to be sometimes.

Her mother told her that while she was younger, she had seen her grandmother do amazing things with her mind also, but she never saw her moving objects with her mind at will.

Early in her childhood, she realized she was different from others. It is one thing to be told that you were special your whole life;

most parents thought of their children as exceptional, and some even thought their children were better than others. Chelsi, at the time, didn't put total stock in what her mother told her. Her mother didn't want everyone outside her immediate family to know her abilities, and her parents took great pains maintaining secrecy. At the time, she was scared of her powers, which felt like they were growing daily. She sensed, even then, that she was capable or would be capable of performing other abilities, though she didn't know what powers would eventually emerge. The knowledge of other gifts always felt hidden in her subconscious recesses. She started to make an effort to work to master her emotions and situational awareness. She could not afford to slip. Over time, the moving of objects settled down, though she knew she could still move things with her mind. She was confident she could improve her ability with enough practice and focus. Each day she tried to learn more about herself and what her gifts might be able to do.

It was nearly two years after her initial discovery of her gifts when she began to feel something new start up within her. A peculiar tingling sensation set into her body on some mornings, particularly around the edges of her vision. There were times when she'd wake in the middle of the night and see strange shadows dancing before her eyes. At first, her father had suggested she try taking a sleep aid because he was worried about her. After months of being unable to sleep without having vivid visions of things happening in the world around her, Chelsi finally convinced him that her gift was not just her imagination running wild. Her ability to dream vividly had been well documented by her parents since she was old enough to remember. Now, however, there were aspects of the dreams that she did not recognize. They would come to her during the daytime, too, but never so clearly as they appeared while she slept.

She also discovered that her ability to control her emotions was becoming more difficult. She still had her days of frustration, anger, and tears, but more often now those feelings seemed to wash over her in waves rather than coming all at once. When she was upset, her body tended to run hot and cold at the same time. Sometimes she'd find herself shivering on the inside out of pure rage, and other times she would break out in a sweat, seemingly from fear. The oddest part of this was that it seemed to happen almost randoml. And more rarely still, she quickly learned that she needed to stay calm if she wanted to maintain control of her gift.

Her parents didn't know how to handle her situation. Her father was supportive, and his help kept her sane through many trying times, but her mother was terrified. Chelsi's power frightened her. Her own mother was afraid of her. To her, Chelsi wasn't special, she was dangerous. She was sure that her daughter could hurt someone accidentally, perhaps even kill them. She didn't understand how Chelsi couldn't feel the same way. She knew her daughter, and she knew that Chelsi was kind and caring. Even with these fears, she loved her child unconditionally.

As Chelsi grew older, her abilities continued to grow, and the visions she experienced grew increasingly disturbing. One night, as she slept, she saw a man die. He fell to his knees in agony and let out a scream. Then he cried, "No! Please no!" His head bent back, and blood poured from a hole in the center of his forehead!. What made Chelsi cry was the look of horror on his face. The image stayed with her for days, and she was haunted by it for years. She was sure she had killed someone, but she couldn't remember who or why. That fact weighed heavily on her conscience.

Other images followed: people dying in the streets, children being snatched away, and fires burning across the countryside. The only good news was that the visions never came with specific details. She could tell they weren't real, because she could see their faces clearly, and she hear their voices. But she could never tell where the events happened or anything else. Everything was hazy, like it was happening in another place, or maybe a different time.

The visions were terrifying, but they were also exciting. For the first time, she was seeing people and places she hadn't known existed, and it filled her with a sense of wonder. She knew she was witnessing something important, and that her gift was allowing her to see it. She wondered if any of the others in her family had the same ability, though she knew the gifts were inherited, and she would discover more about her heritage when she looked deeper into her mother's side of the family. She planned to explore the possibility, but she was afraid of what she might find. She was afraid of knowing more about her past and having to face whatever it was she had done.

So, she decided to keep her abilities secret, and her secrets to herself. It was easier to accept her gifts if nobody else knew about them. Still, there were times when she longed to talk to someone about what she had seen. She knew she shouldn't feel that way, that she should remain silent and live with her burden alone. But there were times when she wished someone understood what she was going through. She knew that she was not alone, but she felt trapped in her secret life, and that isolated feeling was harder for her to bear than the memories themselves.

When Chelsi reached the age of eighteen, she moved out of her parents' home and went to college. Her parents were disappointed in her decision, but they helped her pay for school. The night she left, Chelsi gave her mother a hug and whispered in her ear, "I love you." She turned toward her father and said, "Thank you for everything," then she and her father slipped out the door and headed for the bus station.

She had never been far from home before, Chelsi thought on the drive. As they pulled up to the bus station, she thought back to her childhood home, when she noticed her father staring at her quizzingly.

"What are you thinking about?" he asked.

"I was thinking about our house. It will be so empty now, without me," she answered.

He laughed, and replied, "It sounds like you miss the house more than me."

They sat in silence for a few moments, and then he said, "I'm proud of you, mija. You're going to do great things someday."

Chelsi smiled and said, "I hope so."

"You'll be fine. Just think about what you can do. Not the bad stuff. Think about how you can help people and make the world a better place."

Chelsi nodded and said, "I just want to help people the normal way, like community service or something, not, you know."

Then she leaned forward and hugged her dad, and she didn't want to let go.

He opened the passenger door for her, and they hugged again. Then he walked to the driver's side, climbed in, and drove away

For four years, she kept her secret hidden. She worked hard at school, and she took care of her responsibilities, and spent as much time as possible with her friends and family. She rarely ever missed dinner or a holiday celebration, and when she did, it was to visit her grandparents. They were her best friends, and they had been by her side her whole life. She loved them dearly, and she knew they loved her just as deeply.

With time, the "Other" had quieted, but only a little. It was always there, on the fringes.

What Chelsi didn't tell anyone, till this day, was that sometimes her visions came true. She would hear random people, her friends or coworkers, talk about things they watched on the news or heard from people in the vicinity of the events, someone whispering in a crowded room. She would tune into the various television news channels; the news story narratives would play out just how they played out in her visions! She would know details of the crimes that weren't reported on the news programs! The pictures and videos would look just like she had dreamt them! Because of this, Chelsi was always looking over her shoulder; she never told anyone about her premonitions; what would they think? She started to become very intuitive about the people around her. It became tough for people to lie to her or disguise their true feelings or intentions. She began to "feel" things. A person's anger, resentment, or aggression toward her. She could feel the good emotions also. Her mother and father's love, for example, but the negative feelings came more accessible to her. At times, she didn't know if that sensing negativity easier in people than positivity spoke to the state of humanity or her own emotional state.

She never saw her abilities not as a part of her, like in those cheesy movies and books. These abilities seemed . . . separated from her, almost like she was two different beings in one body. Since they seemed like they belonged to another being, when she was about fourteen, she named them "The Other." She couldn't explain why she made that name choice; it just made it easier to reconcile living with this "other" thing inside her.

***

Wynwood, evening

Where most saw run-down warehouses in a crime filled Miami industrial neighborhood, Goldman Properties envisioned a retail and cultural hub.

Over twenty years later, it's clear that the vision for Wynwood wasn't unfounded. Located west of Miami Beach and minutes from downtown Miami's clubs and glittering high-rises, this former gritty warehouse district was once home to various car shops, wholesale garment shops, run-down factories, and other industrial establishments.

It was now known as the most vibrant, and culturally rich place in Miami. A lively entertainment district with artwork, restaurants, breweries, clothing stores, dance venues, and live events.

Christine Bradford loved art, so when she got the opportunity to go with her friend to visit the district of Wynwood in Miami, she knew she couldn't pass it up. The area was known as one of the coolest arts districts in the nation; a haven for artists from all over the world who were drawn to its creative vibe and thriving nightlife.

"It's like going back to Paris," said Christine. She had been to Paris many times before, but this place was more like what she imagined it would be like if it still existed; an enclave filled with artists, musicians, writers, poets, chefs, and other creative types. It was a true melting pot of culture and creativity that drew people from all walks of life.

They arrived late on Friday night and were greeted by hordes of people, most dressed in their favorite vintage outfits or in trendy clothes that stood out from the crowd. There were men wearing leather vests, women wearing scarves wrapped around their heads, tattooed guys showing off their piercings, while others wore jeans and T-shirts. They all came together in a joyful celebration of artistic expression and appreciation.

Christine had never seen anything like it; it reminded her of the early days at the gallery, when they first opened their doors and invited everyone into their space to see the new work. Now she felt like she was part of something bigger than herself and wanted to soak it up and experience everything she could. She wasn't sure how long she'd be able to stay, but she didn't want to miss any of it.

"I can't believe I'm here!" she exclaimed. "This is amazing!"

"Yeah, I know! Look at all these great shops and restaurants." Her friend pointed to several places that looked interesting. One of them had a large window display featuring a huge painting of a woman wearing nothing except for a pair of high heels and a small piece of cloth covering her nipples. Christine leaned closer to get a better look and gasped. The woman's torso was painted completely black from head to toe, but her face was hidden behind a mask.

"Whoa!" she said, surprised by the provocative nature of the painting. "What do you think?" asked her friend.

She glanced back at him and noticed he was looking at his phone again. He seemed distracted, not really paying attention to anything.

"I don't know . . . it's strange. It looks like the artist is trying too hard."

Her friend shrugged. "That's art for you. You either love it or hate it."

They walked past the window display and continued down the street, admiring some more pieces of art as they went. Christine loved the way the artist used bold colors and shapes to create abstract images that made no sense, but still managed to convey emotion and feeling. Some were funny, some were sad, and others were frightening. She stopped and stared at one painting that showed a man holding a gun to a woman's head. She pointed to the image.

"You're kidding me! That's supposed to be funny?"

He nodded. "I guess. I just don't understand it. Why would anyone want to paint something like this? It seems so . . ."

"Uncomfortable?" she finished for him.

"Exactly."

They passed another display that featured a series of paintings with dark and disturbing themes. Christine shuddered when she saw one painting of a man sitting on top of a pile of dead bodies. She glanced at her friend and saw that he had also paused to take a look at the image.

"Jesus Christ," she muttered under her breath. "Are we in the right place?"

At that moment, a group of five women walked past them. Each of them was dressed in a revealing outfit that left little to the imagination. Their skin was painted white, and their eyes were covered with red tape, leaving only their mouths exposed. They carried neon signs that spelled out the words "LUST", "FEAR" and "LOVE". They moved their arms and hands rhythmically as they strutted down the sidewalk.

Christine looked at her friend. "Do you think these women are acting?"

He shook his head. "No, they're definitely real. I've never seen anything like this before."

Christine was going to be a famous painter one day. The road had been a challenging one to get where she was now. She knew she still had a long way to go before getting to the place she wanted to be in the world. Being artistic through high school and loving her art classes the most, led her to attend art school after graduating.

Christine still remembered the utter disappointment on her parents' faces when she told them she wanted to go to the Maryland Institute for Art, instead of Yale to study law like her parents had always envisioned for her. Her father almost forbade her from attending art school. He was a lawyer, and his father before him practiced law. He viewed it as the noblest profession a person could aspire to work in. He couldn't understand why his only daughter didn't want to carry on the family business. If it wasn't for her mother talking to him later when he calmed down, her college journey would have been over before it started. Her mother just wanted her only child to live her best life and be happy.

Fortunately, it all worked out; still, she was surprised at how stressful her first year was. Christine would be the first to bust the myth that art students are just chillin' at school all day, drawing and painting for fun. She spent just as much time doing work for her studies as her friends in other fields attending traditional colleges were doing. Just like regular college students, she stayed up way too late doing homework and drank way too much coffee. She remembered one all nighter, when she confused her coffee cup with the paint water cup and got a nasty surprise!

So here she was, taking a much needed summer vacation, and what better place to decompress, shake her ass, and party than Miami!!

That wasn't her only reason for coming here, of course. She wanted to go through the journey of walking through the streets, letting them take her on an artistic journey of the senses and be enveloped in street art while she stumbled into local shops and eateries.

And that was precisely what she was doing when she captured the attention of The Beast.

***

CHAPTER 4

LA ROUGE MIAMI

"I guess it was times like these when you found out who your true friends were," Christine thought. She just needed another thirty minutes to an hour to finish exploring the various art and souvenir shops before she would be game to go to La Rouge Miami.

She and her friends had discussed going to the club early to avoid the long lines that Miami clubs were known for on Saturday nights. They complained that they had looked at murals all day and that it was not safe to walk around lowly populated streets because it was starting to get dark, and while there were a large number of people on the streets, crime was known to happen at night here. An argument ensued, and it was grudgingly, mutually agreed that it would be better for everyone if Christine went and did her thing while they headed to the La Rouge. She would wait in the obscenely long line if she had to. Also, some time apart from the group would be better for everyone to cool their tempers, which was left unsaid. On the outside, Christine had stoically agreed to the terms. Still, when she headed out to go into just a few more stores and take just a few more pictures of the beautiful works of art in the decorated Wynwood, she thought that ONE of them would change their mind and accompany her, even if it was out of pity so that she wouldn't be out on these streets alone.

Well, that didn't happen.

So . . . here she was, walking by herself. She wasn't that worried; she would do what she mostly came here to do, then join her friends to happily gyrate to Hip Hop music till closing and take multiple shots of whatever drink they wanted to buy her, only to regret it the following day. "Hey, that's what Miami vacations were all about!! Right?' she thought to herself.

It didn't become clear to her until later, until it was too late, that a deer away from the herd was easy prey.

Christine took out her phone to look at her Google navigation app; it showed she was fifteen minutes away from Wynwood Walls, an attraction she saw in the magazine on the flight to Miami.

Every artist in the world wanted to leave their mark on Wynwood. Eyes from around the world were on this warehouse district. Having your work displayed at Wynwood Walls meant a lot of people would see it; it didn't matter what kind of artist you were. The collections constantly changed, though a few of the murals were permanent. A mural would usually remain on display for up to three years. She told herself that when she made it big, she too, would be given the honor of displaying her artwork there.

She was about to cross a street when a hand roughly gripped her right shoulder! Christine's blood turned ice cold! She turned around to find the source of the intrusion. Three men stood around her, leering at her. They all looked like they had one shot of tequila, too many. One of them was black, and the other two were white. All three didn't look older than twenty-one. "They probably thought they were going to get some easy tourist ass tonight." Christine thought. And they may well get some tonight, but not from her. Though she dressed provocatively, again, why not, she still had dressed practical enough for walking around; she didn't want to think how painful her feet would be if she had decided to put high heels on. The other girls made the opposite decision, which would probably account for why they didn't want to walk around every part of Wynwood to look at the different scenes of artistic beauty displayed.

"What you gettin' into tonight, shawty?" the black guy asked. She really didn't have time for this. For the second time tonight, she wished somebody would have come with her to the murals. These men could easily overpower her if it came down to it. "Don't be scared now, YOLO!" he said, coming closer and trying to put his arm around her shoulder.

"I'm not scared!" She snapped at him as he moved in closer and leaned towards her ear. "You're a little too close." She took his hand off of her shoulder and stepped away from him.

"Hey!" The man shouted, his eyes wide open and hurt as well. He was clearly shocked by the fact that she had rejected his advances so quickly. "Now look who's being rude!"

He looked over at the other two men standing beside them. They both had smiles on their faces and were waiting for him to continue. They knew they'd gotten under her skin and were eager to see how she responded.

"Look, I don't know what y'all are thinking here but . . ." she started. Her voice sounded small and unsure compared to his own. The words just weren't coming out right. It wasn't like her to be so passive.

The men all laughed. One of them held up his hands in surrender. "Hold on there. We ain't tryin' to be rude here. Just having some fun. You shouldn't be afraid o' us though. We ain't gonna do anythin' to ya. You know we don't want no trouble. Ya hear?"

The tall one spoke again. "Why don't you let us help ya out? We can give ya a ride back home. Make sure you get home safe."

"No thanks," she replied, not wanting to go anywhere with these guys. They were clearly looking for trouble.

She turned and walked away from them, starting to walk toward the street. The three men followed behind her a few steps.

"What you talkin' bout girl? We got money. We'll take care of ya. Don't gotta worry 'bout nothin'."

"Just go. I've already told you what's going to happen."

They continued to follow her, and she could tell that they were getting angry at her refusal to accept their offer. Christine decided to ignore them.

She saw very early that course of action wasn't going to work.

The signal to cross the street couldn't have come fast enough. Christine thought she was free of her pursuers, then she turned around to see that the group was following her across the street; they weren't taking no for an answer!

"Where you going, girl? Why you acting all stuck up and bougee!?" The taller white guy called. "We just want to show you a good time; where your homegirls at?" He asked.

Christine quickened her pace; when she first realized who they were, she was nervous; they seemed harmless, but now this was getting serious! Where was a cop when you needed one?

Christine started to accelerate her pace to an in-between walk and run. Now they were whistling at her. They were also beginning to close the distance between them. Christine saw a dark alley ahead that went to the right. It was EXACTLY the alley that you absolutely DID NOT enter the movies, but she didn't have many options to lose these guys. Maybe they watched the same films she did. She would breeze rapidly through the alley and hope there was a cop nearby if this group decided to follow her through the passage.

The alley was dimly lit, but she could clearly see the bright light of the street on the other end. SHE JUST HAD TO MAKE IT TO THE OTHER SIDE TO THE LIGHTS!

She was running at a full sprint; she wasn't stopping to dawdle as the alley's darkness started to close over her. She was halfway through when something hard on her right side sent her sprawling into the wall.

"What the fuck just happened?" Christine thought as she attempted to get up after being flung onto the painted wall. She didn't have to worry about expending the energy to stand up because she was abruptly lifted by her neck to the point that the tips of her toes were scraping the ground.

Then she felt the worst pain she had ever felt or would feel, in her life, penetrate like a knife into the middle of her back!

She could hear and feel something in her back break and give way to what felt like knife cutting edge, totally bisecting her vertebrae in a slow, sick, sawing motion. She started rapidly whimpering and breathing.

"No, no, NOOOOOOOO!"

Then she ceased whimpering and breathing, and before she could get a scream out, the connection to her lungs, diaphragm, and extremities was gone.

"What the fuck did you do to her!" she heard the group leader following her earlier yell.

She was let go by the force and fell limply to the ground. Her body dropped to the ground like a marionette whose strings had been cut. She still had feeling in her face and could feel the liquid that was her life's blood pooling around her. She heard tennis shoes rapidly run away from the visage, along with all hope. The last thing she saw before she expired was the darkness covered by a hoodie looking down at her; it was faceless. The only thing she could see in that darkness was intense, golden, and yellow eyes!

***

Wynwood, evening

Jake thought he was a good-looking guy; any one of these bitches should be happy he was taking to the time to act interested in them. High school was an excellent time for him. His good looks and athletic ability enabled him to breeze through high school and secure a football scholarship at Texas A&M, despite making mediocre grades. Texas A&M was the clear choice for him, even though he had gotten offers that included a football scholarship from other Universities. Jake was from Texas and loved Texas; he didn't want to live anywhere else.

He had heard about the summer party scene in Miami; women came from all over the world to tan by the beaches, eat the food, and hook up with guys they hardly knew in places like Wynwood. "Perfec!!" Jake thought that was precisely what he wanted. Maybe he would get lucky and bag a hot Cougar sugar mama; the money he was getting from his parents barely accommodated the lifestyle he had grown accustomed to at the college. He and his bros had saved up most of their money to make this trip. His parents wanted to see him during his vacation, but he lied to them so he could come here, claiming that he would stay on campus to get in shape and prepare for the new term. He felt guilty when he thought back on it. He had good parents who he knew loved him and wanted to see him fulfill his potential, but he was young and had to sow his wild oats while he had time, before starting his career in the NFL.

Bagging a Cougar, or any girl, for that matter, was proving more complicated to do than he and his crew originally planned.

It seemed to him that every girl tonight that he or his boys attempted to proposition had flatly turned them down. Did every woman that crossed the Georgia-Florida line suddenly become a

Diva instantly? He and his boys were drinking a lot; that is what you do when you are on vacation! Jake had no problems in the women department back home; girls threw themselves at him on campus.

Jake and his boys were feeling very irritable by the time they got around to propositioning Christine. She was having none of it, but Jake would not give up.

When he and his friends followed that girl to the alley, he wished to God that he had given up on her when he had the chance. Jake couldn't believe what he was seeing, this bitch had him messed up!

There she was, sprinting down the alley at full speed when something hit her from the right and sent her flying toward the wall! He saw just a flick of movement. Whoever or WHATEVER it was that hit her, had moved inhumanly fast; he had seen only a flicker of movement! Then whatever it was picked her up with one hand by the neck like a newborn baby and faced her toward the group! Next, he heard what he thought were crunching sounds that caused the girl's body to jerk and convulse uncontrollably, almost like she was being sawed in half! Was that bone being broken, he heard, or worse, cut? He could see portions of the thing doing the damage; It was wearing jeans and a hoodie. A bodybuilder's muscular physique almost tore out the hoodie and jeans. He couldn't see a face, but the hand holding the girl's neck was nearly the size of her head! The appendage had red hair that covered the knuckles and long nails, or claws would be a better word, that were more than two inches long! Jake was terrified, and what terrified him the most was not its size or even its strength. Bright, yellow, and gold eyes were all that could be seen from the seemingly infinite darkness that obscured the face inside of the hoodie! They seemed to almost want him to intercede on her behalf, DARED him to intercede on her behalf! Their brightness and intensity almost hypnotized him.

Then it smiled at him, slowly cutting the girl in half like it had all the time in the world.

The rest of them all came running, but there was nothing they could do, not even if they wanted to get involved, because everyone knew the law here, and if you got caught doing anything against the laws of the city, no matter how small, you'd be screwed for sure! Especially since the girl was unconscious and probably dying, and so far none of them had seen who did this to her. If anyone was going to get blamed for this, it would be them!

"Oh my God," one of Jake's friends yelled as he witnessed the carnage. "I think that bitch is dead!"

Sharp, ivory teeth appeared between the jaws, its tongue moved around its mouth, and saliva dripped from its lips, with two larger canines protruding out in the front in an arrogant smile! The smile was mocking him, its eyes LAUGHING at him!

"We need to get the fuck out of here!" Another one of Jake's friend yelled.

So that's what they did. They ran away from the killer as fast as possible, knocked other tourists down, and almost got hit by more than a few cars a few times making their escape! They never called for help. When they returned to their hotel, they didn't call the police; they didn't want to be implicated or involved. They instead choose to bear their guilt and cowardice in silence. Though they never spoke of what they saw in that alley, none of them would ever forget those yellow and gold eyes of the Beast for as long as they lived!

***

Chapter 5

Chelsi, Homestead

Chelsi kept running; she dared not look behind her to see what was pursuing her. She could hear Its heavy breathing, though she felt no. . .knew, that it wasn't breathing hard because of the exertion of the chase!

It was excited. It reveled in the thrill of the hunt.

She had the impression that it could have easily caught up with her and ripped her apart ages ago if it wanted to. It was playing with her like a cat plays with a mouse before it closes in for the kill.

Her body was near exhaustion. Only fear and the primal pull of self-preservation kept her moving at this point.

If she had her wits about her and wasn't focused on putting one foot in front of the other, she may have reacted better to what came next.

She felt the ground disappear from under her. She was floating through the sky for a minute, weightless.

She fell directly into a pool of blood and flesh!

The coppery taste of blood and small solid objects flooded her mouth and nostrils. When she fell into the pool, she didn't have the presence of mind to close her mouth. When she opened her eyes in the blood, all she saw coagulated swirls of red and black! She immediately swam upward; while she swam, she could feel solid objects bump into her, and she didn't want to think about what they were. When she broke the surface, she aggressively started coughing the blood out of her airway. She attempted to clear the blood from her eyes but couldn't rub out the substance; she needed her arms and legs to tread and keep her head above the liquid. She then started swimming in the direction she HOPED was the direction she was running from. It was the LAST direction she wanted, but it was her only reference point. If she kept swimming in the same direction, she had to hit solid ground eventually, right?

She made it to solid ground.

When she felt the blessed earth, she crawled out of the muck, leaving a long, greasy slick of gore and blood behind her that trailed from the pool. She coughed more of the pool contents out of her mouth and was about to go to work clearing her vision when she realized she was not alone.

She could hear its breathing, so close that she could almost feel its breath on her. Then the Beast roughly picked her up by the neck and sank its claws into her back!!

Chelsi awoke screaming and covered with sweat. That same nightmare had invaded her sleep again.

The nightmares were slightly different every time, but they all ended the same way. She was being chased by the Beast in a forest, and the Beast always got her in the end.

Were these dreams trying to tell her something? If so, then what? Her dreams had revealed events in real life before. Was there a wild animal out there terrorizing South Florida? She needed to talk to her *Abuela*.

Chelsi lay in her bed for another twenty minutes. She REALLY didn't want to deal with this today. She finally dragged herself into the shower to clean off the sweat and other things. She recalled swimming in the pool of blood, which made her feel dirty; she could still feel the blood, excrement, and pieces of flesh on her body and hair.

Cubans mostly settled in and around Downtown Miami after the Cuban Revolution in the 1950s and 1960s. The U.S. government established the Freedom Tower, known then as the Miami News Tower, in those days, to provide additional funding and government programs for refugees fleeing political or religious persecution after the 1962 Migration and Refugee Assistance Act were passed.

Thousands of Cubans settled in and around the tower and Downtown in an attempt to transition into American life. Over time, they eventually branched out and settled into other nearby areas, including west of downtown, which would ultimately become known as "La Pequeña Habana" or "Little Havana."

Little Havana is where Chelsi's grandmother, Alejandra Molina, called home.

Abuela is a true Original Gangster! Chelsi thought.

In the decades that followed, the community started near downtown Miami had started moving across Miami-Dade County to cities like Hialeah and areas like Kendall, Westchester, and other stretches of Southwest Miami-Dade; her grandmother had decided to stay at the first place she lived in America after she fled the Castro regime in Cuba.

Waves of immigrants and history have left their watermark from street to street in these Miami neighborhoods; they were as different as the multicultural people who live in this subtropical metropolis,

It was said by many that if you wanted to experience the heart of the Magic City, you should follow the aroma of the fresh-brewed Café Cubano, or the rhythms of *pachanga* that permeated the streets of Little Havana.

In recent decades, Nicaraguans from Central and South America have settled in Little Havana. These entrepreneurs had established *fritangas*, or cafeteria-style restaurants, and had even named a street after Nicaraguan poet Ruben Dario; despite these migrations, the Cuban imprint remained strong in Little Havana.

Chelsi loved walking down old Calle Ocho; it was the epicenter of Little Havana. Walking down Calle Ocho always made her feel like she had been transported to the Caribbean Islands, or Central and South America.

She loved the artwork, the Walk of Fame, and the giant rooster statues. She enjoyed the food and the welcoming people. The cigar operations were fascinating also. When she had the time, she would check out the Bay of Pigs Monument, or Domino Park, where many elders come to relax and play dominos.

The smell of Cuban coffee, roasted plantains, fried yucca, and carne asada wafted from every restaurant window. She could hear salsa music coming from the bars and clubs that lined the street. But it wasn't just smells and sounds that made her feel like she was in a foreign place. It was also the people. They were all so different—like a rainbow of colors on an endless spectrum of humanity, with no two alike.

She liked the way they dressed too: bright colored shirts and colorful skirts with embroidery that looked like it had been sewn by hand. Or the men's pants with frayed cuffs, high-waisted, and worn-out at the knees. For women, there were brightly patterned dresses or blouses over jeans. Men wore knee-length shorts with embroidered vests and scarves around their necks. And everything—from the clothes to the jewelry to the food to the houses—was so colorful.

She would have loved to live here. In fact, she wondered why she hadn't already. Maybe it was because she was afraid that would mean she would be constantly around people, bombarded with their mental whispers and emotions? Would she get used to it eventually? Was she really strong enough? Did she want to find out?

When she came across a shop that sold cigars, she had to walk past it. She couldn't help but imagine herself lying on a hammock on the balcony of one of the colorful houses, smoking a cigar and drinking rum while her children played on the porch below. She'd listen for their giggles and cries as they ran around playing tag or hide-and-seek.

What would her life be like if she lived here? What would her kids' lives be like, if she ever had any? How would she do it? Could she stay here without being surrounded by the voices of others all the time? Would she even want to?

Her thoughts started to wander again when she walked past another shop displaying a sign that read "Paraíso."

"Paradise?" Chelsi thought to herself. "That's not what I'm looking for right now."

Her grandmother's apartment was a few blocks from the strip. When she called her to ask to visit, her grandmother could not disguise the excitement in her voice at the prospect of seeing her only granddaughter.

The last time they were in each other's company was a few months ago. Chelsi's job didn't give her much time to visit people. When you initially walked into the old apartment, it looked like any other dwelling an older lady living by herself would look like.

The apartment was homey and comfortable. Chelsi had many happy memories as she grew up when her mother would bring her here to visit her family. It was Chelsi's home away from home. When you entered the house, the smell of Cuban food and cleaning products attacked your nostrils. Her grandmother had a typical living room. There were two couches, a chair, and a table in the center. The couches were dark maroon, and the center table was glass with gold-painted metal legs. There was a brown carpet; the mixture of the furniture, walls, and carpet made the room dark. The television's top was used as a mantle that held family photos. Although the living room was comfy, Chelsi's grandmother had put the room off-limits to everyone when Chelsi was a child.

She still had a record player in the living room she had brought from the old country. It was one of the few possessions they could afford to bring with them.

On the way to the kitchen, you passed through a narrow hallway. The walls through the hallway were littered with color and black and white photographs of Chelsi's mom and her grandfather. Chelsi's Abuela was an only child, and her mother was also an only child. Only when you went into the back room, where few people were allowed to enter, would you know that Chelsi's grandmother was different than ordinary grandmothers.

Chelsi's grandmother was a *Bruja*.

Growing up, Chelsi did not realize that her family practiced Santeria. Her parents never discussed the meanings behind the holy images in her grandmother's back room, and she grew up believing that her family was devoutly Catholic. Although she was fascinated by the altar, her grandmother kept to the Orisha, it was not until a trip to Cuba when she was a child did she get the opportunity to observe the Carifiesta festival that she became truly curious about Santeria.

Cubans brought many traditions from the old country, and Chelsi had been exposed to some of these traditions growing up.

Her mother had told her that many times when parents come to this country, they would get the mixed message that celebrating the old world would keep their children backward. Her mother had died before she traveled to Cuba with her father.

While in Cuba, Chelsi observed the public portion of an initiation into the Santeria priesthood. Chelsi believed she saw her mother's spirit manifested through a medium during a ceremony.

Her spirit manifested startling, frightening . . . comforting things. At first, she didn't believe it; she thought the whole ceremony was an exhibition for her benefit, but the spirit knew things about her that no one else knew. It made Chelsi realize then that though her mother had transitioned to the afterlife, it did not mean she was no longer there. Abuela had explained that Santeria is based on balance, on activating the sacred within. The religion allows one to empower oneself with sacred energy, drawing on the inner sacredness that each person carries as part of their nature.

She was told that it also meant respecting one another and recognizing certain sacred powers would help us all function as a family.

"We see nature as sacred, an extension of ourselves." Abuela had said. "Thus, you can't pollute nature," she continued. "You must maintain it for your own survival. If you disrespect the environment, you're disrespecting yourself, saying you have no value. When a society values money over human life, you've got a problem."

Her grandmother's words made perfect sense, especially since Abuela had brought her up to respect herself, to treat her body well. She hadn't been exposed to much of any religion growing up, but her mother had always talked about how important it was to take care of herself and to be proud of who she was. Her mother hadn't practiced the Santeria, but she believed in it. That made it all the more real for Chelsi.

It was comforting to know that her mom wasn't just gone—she wasn't even dead! She was just somewhere else and she could visit if she wanted. It meant she really was still out there. It meant she had someone looking after her.

Chelsi personally didn't know what to believe, but she couldn't deny that she felt a presence during that ceremony in Cuba long ago. She missed her mother. Chelsi didn't know, but she had always suspected that her mother had gifts like her. She always seemed to know when Chelsi was in distress and always knew what to do or say to make her feel better.

She wondered if the spirits of those who gave their lives for a righteous were still with the living somehow. Maybe they weren't dead at all; maybe they were just more alive than anyone else on Earth. Maybe they would be able to communicate, even from the other side of the veil. Her mind raced through possibilities as she considered what she might have done differently if she'd known then that her mother could do such things. But it wasn't possible to change the past and she couldn't imagine how she would have acted any differently. The truth remained that without her parent's help, Chelsi wouldn't be here today.

***

Little Havana

Alejandra Molina was a distinguished-looking older woman. Chelsi could see where she and her mother got their looks from when she looked at her. Chelsi had seen pictures of her grandmother when she was about her age; she was very striking! The years had been good to her; she looked 20 years younger than her age. While other women her age were struggling with health issues, Alejandra continued to stay active.

She made her living by practicing the art of Santeria. Many in the neighborhood believed that her grandmother could look into one's soul. She could cure illness, ensure healthy offspring, drive away evil spirits, and talk to dead loved ones. People would come almost daily with tributes or donations. Abuela never had to worry about crime. She could go anywhere she pleased in Little Havana and other parts of Miami. She was well known here. Generations of people in Miami grow up with their parents warning them at night before they went to bed, the consequences of angering a *Bruja*! People came from all over, from every walk of life to seek the elderly woman's assistance in spiritual matters.

She had married young, and Alejandra bore one child, Chelsi's mother, Juanita. As a young woman, her husband died at a work accident when they immigrated to Florida, suddenly leaving her alone to raise their daughter. Without even the opportunity for an education, she took on the role as head of the household and sole provider.

Alejandra managed quite well, but it was difficult raising a child by herself. At first Juanita struggled under her mother's harsh discipline. But after the death of her father, she became rebellious.

She would often run off into the streets of Miami without telling anyone where she was going. This only added to her mother's guilt. She knew she should have done more for her daughter. She should have been there for her. She should have tried harder. No matter how much she did, her daughter still rebelled against her. After several attempts at trying to control her rebellious daughter, she gave up and simply let her go. After all, it is not easy to control an adult.

Then came the day that Chelsi's mother died of cancer. Her mother had always been such a strong woman. Even as her body was ravaged by the disease, her spirit remained strong. She stayed strong and confident until the end. In her last weeks, she was so weak that she couldn't get out of bed. It broke Chelsi's heart to see her like that. Juanita had always said that if anything ever happened to her, her grandmother would be there. And so, she was. When Chelsi arrived at the hospital, her grandmother was already there. She sat by her bedside crying. The old woman spoke softly to Chelsi's mother, consoling her as she lay dying. She told her not to fear, for the spirits had sent her granddaughter to help her through this time.

When Chelsi's mother passed away, Alejandra was devastated. Her grandmother showed her many signs, including a hummingbird flying out of nowhere, a red cardinal sitting on a branch outside her window, and a butterfly landing on her shoulder. All these things were meant to tell her that she was being watched over and guided.

As was customary in her family, she began to pray to the spirits asking for guidance. She asked them to show her what she should do with her life. Was she destined to remain here in Miami? Or was it time for her to leave? She went about her daily business while she waited for her answer. One morning she woke up and felt different somehow. Something in the air seemed to change, as though the weight of the world had lifted from her shoulders. She realized that the answer she had sought was right in front of her, it was her mission to protect and mentor her beautiful *nieta*, her grandchild. So she remained in Little Havana. She continued to serve as a *Bruja*, working as a healer and seer. She also served as an influence for good. She helped people who needed her, whether they were rich or poor. She went out of her way to help those around her. As she grew older, she continued to help guide others. She took care of her grandchild and other people's grandchildren, teaching them the ways of the spirits. She taught them to be strong people of great character.

She became something of a legend. People came from all over the world to visit her and pay tribute to her. Some would bring gifts and offerings, others just wanted to share their stories. A few years later, she had become a very popular figure in Miami. People recognized her everywhere, and they stopped whatever they were doing to chat with her. She was a celebrity in Miami.

When Chelsi called her and told her about the visions, it was parallel to what she had been feeling for months now. A great evil was growing in Miami.

"I don't know," she whispered. "This is too big. I am no match for it. I can't fight it alone. I need your help. It's why I called you Abuela. I need you to fight this evil with me!"

Abuela nodded slowly as she held the phone to her ear.

"You are right, Chelsi," she replied. "This is something we must do this together. We are family after all."

She could almost feel Chelsi's relief through the phone. She smiled and thanked her grandmother for everything she had done for her.

***

CHAPTER 6

The Beast

"Last night had been oh so exhilarating!" The Beast thought. Despite the feelings, It knew that hunting in a crowded location was never a good idea. It had gotten lucky with the meat stalked a few weeks ago; the prey was in a more secluded area. It could see its target was having car issues on the Turnpike; The road leading up to this particular exit ramp was relatively straight and easy to navigate. It followed close behind, keeping to the shoulder as best It could when there weren't cars coming from either direction. The Beast's senses were on full alert for any sign or scent of its prey at all times. It stopped following at just the right moment, sensing that its playmate was about to make a turn onto the exit ramp. "Perfect!" the Beast thought as it waited patiently before moving forward once again.

It wasn't long before the girl made the left-hand turn onto the ramp; It took up a position directly across the highway from where the vehicle would be exiting without hesitation. It leaped off the shoulder and into the street, making sure not to leave too much of a trail back to the exit ramp itself, then ran down the ramp, avoiding traffic by running parallel to the road. It rounded the corner and saw the car parked near the end of the ramp. There was no one around. It could not get better than this!

Then the Beast thought about Wynwood, which was a different hunt, a different rush! There were so many ways one could get compromised, but what was life without a bit of risk! Despite the potential of more reckless fun, the Beast knew it could not afford to make a habit out of what happened last night. It was lucky that those cowardly pups tucked their tails and ran when they caught It playing with Its new dear . . . dear friend. The Beast was restless, and not just because of lack of playtime. It sometimes felt that something, or someone, was watching It. The feeling only came when it was stalking, or killing.

When those damnable Salem women had crossed Its path!

The Beast remembered them vividly. The witches who dared to go against It. They must have thought they were so clever at first, but their plans all went south in the end.

How foolish of hem! How blind and stupid!

Its eyes glowed yellow with anger as it from the memory of watching the witch's village burn. It was a terrible shame that their stupidity would cost so many lives.

Those poor, poor souls. The very mortals you swore to protect, in the end, betrayed you! The Beast could not help but feel some measure of *satisfaction at the thought. Did they really think they'd be able to defeat It?*

They were fools who could never understand power! All the things that happened next—the accusations of witches' curses, the villagers' deaths—all of it was just a result of their own hubris. I warned them about this. Warned them of the danger their actions posed. But they didn't listen!! Those silly, stubborn fools! The Beast roared with laughter in Its mind, its anger finally abated.

The Beast's mind returned to the present, to that ever-present fear of being exposed!!! Over the years, It had made a great success of blending in with the cattle. That being said, It knew from experience that there were other beings out there that were special. They were mortal, to be sure, but It had always had a sense that there were those who possessed powers to bring about Its untimely demise. "Just like them," the Beast chided. "I should have been more wary." It started to feel something rise up, an emotion that It thought It hadn't felt in centuries; was it fear? And something else, blissful excitement!!!

Little Havana, Abuela's apartment

"Qué pasa, mi pequeño?" Abuela asked.

"Tengo visiones aterradoras Abú", Chelsi replied. She had come here because she knew that she needed help understanding her nightmares. She knew on some subconscious level, that they were trying to tell her something, but what? This was the first time she had started experiencing recurring nightmares. She had so many questions! What was that animalistic thing chasing her in the forest? Why was it going after her? Was it going after her or was she representing somebody else in visions? She had browsed the news channels like she usually did when she thought she had seen a crime take place in a vision, but she didn't see anything on TV that would even come close to the scenes in her nightmares. Maybe the police were working with the media, intentionally not featuring the details of the murders to flush out the killer. Then she thought maybe there were no murders taking place and she was just losing her mind.

"Cómo puedo ayudar a mi amor?" Abuela asked.

"I think someone out there is doing bad things to people, but I don't know how to stop them," Chelsi said.

Abuela sagely nodded and said, There is a way to track the source of your visions, but are you ready for where that may take you?"

She looked directly into Chelsi's eyes, taking her measure. "You may not be able to go back to life as you know it now; the path of a *Bruja* is at times fraught with danger! Your Mother and I had disagreements about this many times; she did not want that for you. She wanted you to live a normal life. She was scared of her gifts and did her best to hide them from everybody, even her loved ones, but she could not hide them from me, and she could not make the gifts just "go away" because they are a part of us."

Alejandra Molina paused to give Chelsi time to take in everything she was saying. "Just like you couldn't hide yours from her. I must warn you. If we do this, if we open that door, whatever you are looking at may be able to LOOK BACK AT YOU! Despite the dangers, I still believe THAT THIS MUST BE DONE! Péinate o hazte papelilla, mija, you must decide!"

"I don't want to be a Bruja!" Chelsi said a little too aggressively. "I just want to be able to, for once in weeks, get a good night's sleep and stop whoever, or whatever, is doing these horrible things!" She couldn't help but wonder if why she couldn't be normal and just live a boring and normal life. It was an argument she had with herself every day. She glanced over to the window at the end of the room. The curtains were drawn tight as always, but she could still see the faint glow of the streetlight outside through a small crack. Not that it mattered. The curtains are not going to keep out the danger she strongly believed was out there.

"Like I told you," Abuela countered, "you don't choose when to use the gifts; the gifts choose when to use YOU!"

Chelsi didn't want to argue with her grandmother; she shrugged with resignation and asked, "How do we begin?"

***

Miami Beach, evening

Ronald Stanford was bored out of his mind. There were worse ways to earn a living, he grudgingly thought to himself; it paid a lot better than Uncle Sam. He was trained in all sorts of skills with the Agency. Among the skills he learned were anti-surveillance and the security of an asset.

The Agency, not to be confused with the CIA, or Central Intelligence Agency, was a government agency known to few people on the Beltway. The Beltway, is the metropolitan area that surrounds DC, the area that headquartered the Federal Bureau of Investigation, or FBI.

After some event forced him to part with the Agency some years ago, he had to find a way to pay the bills. An old buddy he knew from when he worked with military Special Operations had put him onto his first job in the private security business; Ronald never looked back. To say that the guy he was guarding presently was a scumbag was a gross understatement. He started out as a wanna-be UFC fighter; after his fifth professional loss, he somehow got a spot on a reality TV dating show, where he got kicked off after just five days for homophobic and racist comments. After he was kicked off the show, it took little time for him to find a new way to hustle the unsuspecting masses, becoming a relationship guru. He established a website that offered training courses on accumulating wealth and, to quote what Ronald had read on the internet, "male-to-female interactions!" He then created a platform where he had members pay a monthly membership fee to receive "instruction".

The Client did have the sense, however, to rent a private cabana. The cabana isolated him from the constant in-and-out traffic of the resort from morning to late evening. The Client had bought out the pool areas adjacent to the cabana so that only the people HE wanted to come in would get in, and while this was advantageous for security reasons, it obscured everybody in the area from sight if something went wrong.

There were four guards at the cabana who knew how to stay out of sight unless they needed to interact with someone. One of them sat outside the door twenty-four hours a day, waiting for any indication there might be trouble. If he heard anything suspicious, he'd call one of his fellows inside, and together they'd take care of business. There was another guard inside the cabana, but he didn't sleep; he just stayed awake all night long so he could react quickly when necessary.

The entire place was wired for video. However, it wasn't enough to completely safeguard the place. It simply wasn't possible to secure every inch of a large property. The rest of the guards patrolled the perimeter of the property, and they kept watch over the windows and doors as well. They made sure nobody walked by without being seen or announced. The cabana itself had two cameras: one pointed at the entrance, which covered the front door and the landscaping around it, and one pointing straight down into the cabana. This camera had no blind spot in its field of view.

The camera that was pointed down showed the cabana's interior in full color. That was useful because it let the guards know what was going on inside the cabana, especially important since the Client was known for having several girls working for him at once. He liked to have a variety of women available to entertain his guests. So even though they couldn't actually see anything, they knew where everyone was, and who was doing what to whom. If there was an emergency, these cameras would provide evidence of exactly what happened and when it took place. This meant the guards had to make certain the girls weren't using the cabana for anything other than privacy.

They never found anything out of the ordinary, but they also never expected to. Not with the amount of money involved. The Client always paid top dollar for the best services. And he always paid upfront so there was no reason for anyone to be concerned about losing money.

That said, while most of the women who worked for the Client were professionals, some were not. Some were amateurs who were trying to make their way in the world. Some were pretty, young and naive; others were old, experienced and wise. Those who were not professional prostitutes were smart enough to realize that the Client's main interest was sex, and the more of it they could give him, the better their chances of getting a second date.

It didn't matter what kind of girl you were. As long as you were willing to do whatever he wanted, he was happy.

In fact, the Client preferred it that way. He didn't want to waste time explaining things to a virgin who didn't understand what he wanted. He was too busy running a global empire, and he certainly didn't like to explain his preferences to anyone. But while the Client was perfectly capable of telling a woman what he wanted, he didn't like to talk about it much. Instead, he left that up to the girls who came here.

He paid them well to do whatever it was he wanted, and he told them to leave their morals and ethics behind.

The Client didn't care what the girls did to each other. He didn't care if they hurt one another. All he cared about was getting laid.

"I thought we told the staff that NO ONE could come up to the cabana entrance area without first running it through security as the figure approached, fucking amateurs!! The first bodyguard thought to himself."

The first bodyguard didn't have time to bring his mic up to his mouth or pull out his pistol before he was slashed across the throat by the Beast. The second guard thought he heard something but didn't go to investigate; what he HAD heard was the heels of the first guard scraping the ground as his body was being dragged into the nearby tropical foliage, blood still squirting out of his neck. The second bodyguard didn't think that anything was amiss. He thought the other bodyguard was probably taking a piss in the plants or something. They had worked together for years. He knew his colleague was solid. Besides, they were all armed with brand new Glock 17's and could communicate at a moment's notice if shit got hairy. All the same, the second bodyguard was a professional, so he conducted a radio check on the first bodyguard.

"Sentinel one, this is Sentinel two, radio check," the second bodyguard spoke into his mic. No answer. He checked in with the third bodyguard, who promptly replied, then tried getting through to the guard at the cabana collocated with the Principal.

"Sentinel four, this is Sentinel two." He said into the mic.

"Sentinel two, this is Sentinel four; I read you Lima Charley," Sentinel four replied.

Ronald had briefly been with the team, but he seemed ok. He didn't talk about his past too much and stayed to himself. Sentinel Two had heard that Ronald had been a door kicker for the Agency back in the day before taking up private security. He had heard Ronald was a major badass, so why was he slumming it here with us? Sentinel Two shrugged. Whatever issues Ronald had in his past, at this job his head was always on a swivel, and he always conducted himself as the consummate professional; that's all you could ask for!

Sentinel Two thought all this as a claw shot out of his chest from his back. He would never think of anything after that. When the third bodyguard was attacked, he rapidly felt the ground come up from below him and didn't realize that his left leg below the knee had been ripped off until the back of his head hit the solid ground. That recognition interval lasted only seconds before his head was crushed like a watermelon by the force of the claw.

"That was far too easy!" the Beast thought. It didn't know why It had chosen this playground tonight, or correctly, it was never in the Beast's plan. On one of the rare nights It watched the television, the Beast had tuned into a news documentary about a man who seemed like a fellow hunter if the documentary was true. This man was a longtime hunter of weak women and fools.

Delicious, thought the Beast, who could always make the time to appreciate the work of a fellow professional! Another news channel featured the man frequenting different locations around Miami a few months later. The Beast couldn't believe Its luck! The Beast knew that there would be others guarding this man.

Oh what a delight and a challenge it would be to rip HIM apart, the Beast thought. A man with this much infamy would not be around the public eye. The Beast could empathize with that! It had then spent three days driving around Miami before It found him. Once It got the quarry's scent and what vehicles were being used, it was an easy matter of following his entourage's movements to the resort. The Beast had followed the targets' path from their hotel room to the pool area where they had taken up residence near the bar and grill. Then It had spied on them all night until It decided to creep back inside.

Its prey had been careless enough for It to have gotten this far without notice! Now all It had to do was wait until they were asleep so It could make its move. It was nearly midnight now. They would all be exhausted and more vulnerable than usual. The Beast smiled as It made Its final preparations. All It needed was two hours. That should be plenty of time.

The Beast crept out of the shadows towards the poolside lounge where Its prey had sat earlier. It paused at the edge of the pool, gazing down upon the scene below. The beach was lit by the moonlight, casting a blue tint over everything except the water itself. The water was calm, but the waves lapped against the shoreline intermittently. The only sounds were the gentle sounds of the ocean, and the occasional chirps of crickets and frogs from the nearby trees. There was no one in sight. The Beast gazed upon the scene, making sure It wasn't being watched before continuing forward. It moved along the ground, crouching down as It approached the pool. As It neared the lounge, the Beast heard a faint noise coming from behind some shrubbery just ahead of It. It stopped briefly to listen, but when nothing else occurred, It continued forward. Taking the three guards out had been anticlimactic, to say the least, but the Beast didn't have all night; this would have to be quick and fast. That's why it was always a bad idea to go after the Playmates recklessly! The Beast's heightened senses reached out to find Its quarry. It could smell and hear only two heartbeats left. The Beast deduced that one of them was a guardian by the smell of cotton, polyester, gun oil, and sweat. So that meant the other one was It's new Playmate!

***

CHAPTER 7

MIAMI BEACH, EVENING

Ronald was posted with his back to the cabana, in a position where no one could come up behind him, and he had clear lines of sight. That wise precaution gave him a few seconds more to react to the intruder than the other poor bodyguards, which ultimately saved his life. With a swift movement gained from years of close-fire engagement training and combat experience, Ronald drew his pistol, aligned his sights, and fired three rounds at . . . he didn't know what it was! All he knew at this point was that whatever it was, he had hit it at least once! It howled and managed to get a blow in on Ronald with its right claw, grazing Ronald on the left forearm.

The three rounds, unfortunately, didn't stop whatever it was from flinging Ronald into the pool! The last thing Ronald thought as he hit the water was how could something so big move so fast? It was like being tossed around inside a washing machine!

It took a few moments for Ronald's mind to adjust to the cold shock of the pool water. He quickly realized that if he stayed under too long, he would drown, but he know if he surfaced too soon, he would be as good as dead. He saw the red form looking down at him from the surface. As the Beast slowly rose to its feet, he instinctively held his breath, because it looked like the Beast was about to pounce on him. He saw a pair of shining yellow eyes staring down at him. Then as suddenly as they came, the eyes disappeared from Ronald's sight. Ronald knew that he would have to figure out something soon, because he was about to drown. He felt himself drifting away from consciousness . . .

The Client was relaxing in the plush bed located in the cabana. He could have easily chosen to lounge in his suite, but he enjoyed the fantastic Miami air tonight and the sounds of the waves crashing onto the beach nearby. The Client was thinking about what he was going to do tomorrow night. He loved seducing those entitled, dumb wanna-be Instagram models in the clubs. They were fun to fuck and so easy to control once he got them drunk. It would be a shame for him to miss out on all the action though. Perhaps he would make an appearance at one or two of the parties before heading back home. He wasn't going to be able to spend much more time here than necessary anyway because he had some other business to attend to in New York City soon after that.

He never thought it possible, but there was something about this place. The sun, sand, water, and most importantly the women. He hated to admit it, but he couldn't wait to come back again. As he continued staring at his phone's screen, he began typing his next text message.

"What do you think of those ladies?" He asked aloud to himself as he reached for the glass of Scotch on the bedside table. "I'm pretty sure I can get all three of them up here with me."

He brought the phone to his face and looked through the pictures. One girl stood out from the rest. She didn't just look like she belonged in his bed; she practically was. Her long legs led up to her tiny waist which flared out into a surprisingly large chest. His cock stirred slightly under the sheet as he stared at the picture. Not only did she look incredible, but he knew he could take her without any trouble. He always preferred a woman with a little meat on her bones.

"That's a tough decision," he said quietly to himself.

He typed another text and sent it off to the man who had requested these girls. A few minutes later, he received a reply.

"No problem, sir. I'll send over two escorts and an extra maid. Hopefully they will be good enough to satisfy your needs."

The Principal smiled. He hoped that he got a chance to see that red head again. He wanted to know if she was as wild in bed as she seemed to be outside of it.

Even though he had been accused of sexual harassment and assault multiple times, and it was public knowledge that he did so, he still had no shortage of naive, thirsty women pursuing him. It was like

Jay Z said, they weren't saving it for marriage; these bitches out here were saving it for KARATS! Or at least they THOUGHT they were getting KARATS OF GOLD. The Client laughed to himself. The gunshots abruptly shook him out of his stupor. "What?" He asked as he turned toward the sounds. There was a gunshot, then another, and another. His eyes widened as he realized what was happening.

"Oh shit!" He exclaimed aloud in panic.

The shooting stopped. No one came through the door or windows.

He took a deep breath and looked down at the gun that lay on his desk next to him. He hadn't even thought about grabbing it. He closed his eyes and prayed. God, please help me! Please don't let them kill me!

After several long moments without any gunshots, the Client decided not to wait around anymore and ran out of the cabana, he also remembered he owned his own Glock 17 for self-defense. You never knew. He retrieved his pistol from under his pillow, then he looked left and right frantically trying to figure out where he should go.

He came out of the cabana waving his pistol yelling, "What the hell are you shooting at? What's going on?"

Those were the only words the Client had a chance to utter. He barely had a chance to scream or fire his weapon before being ripped apart! He fell, and as he did so, his body was being torn into pieces. The whole scene almost made the Beast laugh with glee as the man's head rolled away from him like a soccer ball. His blood poured across the floor, so much blood it looked like someone had taken red paint and smeared it over everything in sight! His guts and entrails followed, squirming out of the gaping hole that had been his belly button, then his legs stretched out on either side of him like bloody stumps! His arms followed suit, one arm coming up to try and shield his face while the other flopped around as though still trying to grasp something!. At last his torso fell onto the ground beside him with a thud! All of this happened in seconds.

The Beast stood above the carnage as the blood flowed down Its back like a river of crimson, and the blood moved all the way down until it reached the Beast's feet. The Beast bent forward and licked up the blood that had pooled there. It tasted good; fresh and sweet. More importantly, it gave him strength. It allowed him to become stronger, faster, to grow even larger. That blood would fuel the changes inside Its body and make It ever more powerful.

Ronald quickly regained consciousness underwater. He basically had two choices, drown or surface and face whatever the fuck had flung him into the pool! A decision was reached in less than five seconds. As he exploded to the pool's surface, he resigned himself to the clawed hand that would rip his head off; then nothing happened. Whatever it was had gone and had left a big mess.

***

Little Havana
Abuela's apartment, evening

Reggaeton music and the sounds of people in bars, hookah lounges, and clubs could be heard everywhere through the night in Little Havana. Miami is arguably most known for its incredible nightlife. Whether you wanted to go to a swanky cocktail bar, or hit the clubs, you will always be in luck.

Usually, Chelsi loved listening to the sounds of Little Havana at night, but her current attention was focused on the altar in the backroom of her grandmother's apartment. They sat facing each other cross-legged. Chelsi's *Abuela* had a bloody dagger in her hand that looked centuries old. The head of a decapitated chicken and an ancient goblet full of blood lay on the altar. Also on the altar were various porcelain vessels that contained stones of different colors, which Abuela explained were regarded as the literal and symbolic representation of the *Oricha*. Eighteen shells were also displayed on the white table. Statues of Roman Catholic saints adorned the walls of the room.

Abuela had explained tonight's proceeding to Chelsi earlier that day. Offerings, or *ebbó*, were given to the *Oricha*, or ancestral spirits, to a person's own Ori, the spark of human consciousness personified as Orisha, and sometimes to the earth. These offerings included fruit, liquor, flowers, candles, money, or slaughtered animals. Divination was often used to determine the exact nature of the offering; Offerings were regularly given to strengthen the spirits, to thank them, or as a supplication; this was supposed to form a give-and-take relationship with the spirits in the hope of receiving a blessing.

The animal sacrifices were called *Matanza*. Birds or other animals were sacrificed by slitting their throats or twisting and ripping their heads off. Rituals of greater importance involved four-legged animal sacrifices. Some said the killing of animals was a substitute for human sacrifice in the days of the past. There were still rumors and stories of children mysteriously coming up missing in Cuba from years ago. The *Oricha* and *Egun* would then ingest the blood of the sacrifice. The life force would then transfer to the *Oricha*, thus strengthening its *Aché*. The more the animal struggled, the stronger its life force would be.

Abuela fixed her gaze firmly on Chelsi. "Te voy a preguntar una vez más, ¿estás listo para esto?", Abuela asked. "Are you ready for this? Like I warned you earlier, once you go down this road, there may be no going back!" Abuela whispered.

Chelsi paused before answering. She still had a choice. She could keep her mouth shut and live her best life. There was no proof, no proof yet, that anything she saw in her nightmares was ACTUALLY happening or going to happen; they could be just that, bad dreams. Regular nightmares resulting from a lousy sleeping schedule and not enough paid time off for a vacation! These thoughts and others went through her head, but one idea came bubbling up to the surface that superseded all others. In her heart . . . she knew. She couldn't explain it, justify it, or even put it in words; she just knew . . . that these nightmares, no . . . visions, were telling her that something dark and evil was out there, doing who knew what to unsuspecting people! It terrified her, yes, but at the same time she felt a strange sense of purpose. What can I do to help? How can I use my powers for good? The questions whirled in her mind like a kaleidoscope, each piece changing as soon as it formed into more questions.

"I am ready," Chelsi said.

"Ok," Abuela breathed, relieved. Abuela then stood up, went to the altar, reached for the goblet of blood, and poured its contents into one of the porcelain vessels.

Then life as Chelsi know it would be forever changed.

***

CHAPTER 8

MIAMI BEACH, MORNING

"You don't want to go in there."

Those words seemed to float in the air between the homicide detective and the pool area entrance. The deputy that uttered them backed away, looking like he wanted to be anywhere else but here. Detective Simon Nicholls knew he shouldn't ask the deputy questions right away. He would let the deputy get a chance to go get some fresh air and vomit, which he looked like he would do any minute. The cabana crime scene was already being cordoned off by yellow tape. The crime scene, reeking of blood, Tiki torch insect repellant, excrement, and more blood, was cramped with Miami Dade PD uniforms and a forensics unit. All were all taking extra care to avoid cross- contamination. That task, however, was proving to be increasingly difficult with the number of bodies that littered the area.

All three dead private security guards had prior military experience, and years of personal security time under their belts. Simonwas still trying to figure out how ALL three highly trained guards and their client could have been taken out without another party taking casualties or getting wounded. To top it off, security camera footage had been erased. At first, he speculated that this was an inside job. The security firm that employed the guards said there were supposed to be FOUR guards assigned to this detail. Ronald Stanford was at this time designated as a person of interest. The WAY these men were killed brushed away all assumptions of a lone perpetrator, Simon grudgingly admitted to himself. One person was not capable of THIS! Also, there remained a possibility that Stanford had assisted in the killing of these men with some outside help.

The Detective Simon Nicholls had been on the Miami Homicide team for a little over seven years and had never seen anything like this. He recalled reading an article on the primary victim. Didn't he get in trouble some years back for some human trafficking shit in Eastern Europe? Did that mean Romanians, or Russians are responsible for this? They had racked up quite a number of bodies in Miami over the years.

His partner, Jane Goodman, was catching another body downtown. So that left him here, at this posh resort he could never afford to stay in with a cop's salary, feeling itchy and hot in the early Miami morning, working a mass murder crime scene. The owner had called it in—one of the cleaning crew had found the first body hidden in the vegetation. The owner had prattled on in his interview about the noise; he'd thought he had briefly heard screaming. Simon motioned over his shoulder for one of the forensic guys, a kid named Donaldson, to come in behind him.

"Don't touch anything yet, okay?" Simon said. "I wanna get a feel for it first."He walked over to the entrance of the cabana, eyes straining to catch anything that would give him some insight into what happened here. Nothing.

As he stepped closer, a sliver of the Miami sun fell on the victim's head, covered with cuts and gashes, illuminating the long gash across his neck, dried blood caked down toward the collarbone of his headless body. Simon recognized something past the exposed rib cage and viscera hanging out the victim's stomach. A flicker of familiarity snapped at him.

"Shit," he said, eyes scanning the man's face again. This may not be a one-off, not anymore.

He wheeled around. He felt himself heat up; sweat spread over him, prickling his back and face.

This must be wrong, but after considering everything he saw, he knew it was true. He told himself it was totally possible, even here in South Florida. It had to be some sort of coincidence, but those two killings were connected somehow, and that meant there'd been other victims before this one. He also was sure that there would be more to come.

The implications sent a shiver through him. Did they have serial killer on their hands?

He scanned the area again, looking for anything he could use as evidence. There wasn't much—the scene was messy because of the decomposition process already under way, and the killer had taken care not to leave any traces behind. But there was enough to get started, and that was all he needed.

"What happened?" he asked. "Any witnesses you know of?" He looked down at the dead man's face, hoping to find some clue.

"No witnesses," the officer answered, shaking his head. "I haven't seen anything like this before."

"You're sure no one saw anything?"

"We canvassed the neighborhood, and we got nothing."

"Maybe the killer came from over by the beach," Simon suggested. "Did you check near the edge of the water?"

"Yes, sir." The officer nodded. "But no sign of anything unusual."

Donaldson stood behind him, a few inches too close, shadowing his movement. He jerked back, surprised by the detective's quick pivot. Simon looked at the younger man with his teenage-looking face and eager eyes. *The light in your eyes will fade soon, Simon thought. Like the rest of us, you'll become jaded to all this. Just give it some time.*

"Get everyone out of here except the people that have to be here," Simon said, his tone flat, eyes locked on Donaldson, who nodded. "And then get John Abraham on the phone. Fast!"

***

Abuela's home
Little Havana. evening

The visions came so fast that Chelsi thought she would pass out, then she remembered what *Abuela* had instructed her to do.

She had said to BREATHE!!

"BREATHE!" She told herself to not fight the visions. Let them come into you and through you, she remembered.

Thousands of slaves from West Africa cramped together in hulls of ships bound for Cuba; their destiny to work sugar and coffee plantations, that is, if they didn't die of dysentery, smallpox, depression, or outright despair! The cruelty of captain and crew, and sexual exploitation was never ending.

Hundreds of people crowded together with little airflow and even less sanitation. The harsh discipline the slaves received, the routine whippings and thumbscrews, brought tears to Chelsi's eyes. Men dying in bloody battles for independence. Innocent people herded into concentration camps, where thousands would later die. A warship with the flag of a foreign land slowly sinks into the ocean. A new constitution created, bringing religious freedom to all. The island's inhabitants desperately trying to stave off the Spanish, English, French, Dutch, and Belgians, as well as the Americans, who were vying for control. It all climaxed when the Cuban people revolted against the Spaniards. Their struggle took on many forms. Men fought on the front lines. Women fighting to protect their children in vain against the tide of history.

From the void in her mind, Chelsi watched as hundreds of Cubans fought valiantly to rid themselves of the Spanish oppressors. She saw the bodies stacked high in mass graves and the cries of the survivors.

Their struggle took on many forms. Men fought on the front lines. Women fought to protect their homes from invaders. Children ran in fear for their lives. Men and women hid in caves and forests. Finally, the Cubans defeated Spain. They had won!

But their victory was short-lived.

Abuela had warned her, "You can't stop now, Chelsi. You have to go further."

Chelsi looked out at the sea of faces, the endless waves of people, the oceans of blood. She looked out at the blood red sky.

Breathe . . . BREATHE!

The visions were overwhelming her. She had to breathe. She had to control the images, or she would lose them completely.

She closed her eyes and focused on her breath. As she did, a small voice inside her said, "What if I don't want to see all of this?"

"There is no way out of here, Chelsi," Abuela said. "If you don't go deeper, there will be nothing, nothing but oblivion."

Chelsi opened her eyes and looked out at the sea of faces again. "I know. I'm sorry, Abuela."

"It's okay, Chelsi. It's okay."

But it wasn't okay.

Chelsi tried to keep breathing, but it became harder and harder. Her vision blurred. She couldn't control her emotions.

Abuela noticed her distress and began to encourage her again. "You can do this, Mija. Go on."

"I'm so scared, Abuela. I don't want to see anymore."

"You must."

"I don't want to see anymore."

"I know, but you must be brave, you must persevere!"

"How can I go deeper? How can I see all of this?"

"You know how, you've always known."

"Why?"

"To make things right, Chelsi. To set everything right. To be a force of justice, like those who came before you!"

"How will seeing all of this heal anything? What can I possibly do with all of this information?"

"That's the question, isn't it? It is the question we all must answer. You can't move forward until you understand why, what you are meant to do with the knowledge you gain."

"So, I'm supposed to tell someone what I've seen? Tell the police what I have seen? What could anyone do with all of this?"

"You have to make it right, there are powers at play beyond the laws of man."

"How can I do that? People will die. There won't be a tomorrow!"

"Yes, some may die."

"They will die because of me."

"Not because of you, Chelsi. Because of what you are meant to do."

"Meaning?"

"Meaning, you must find the truth. You must make it right, and that can only happen if you understand what has occurred. Only then can you prevent the same thing from happening again. Understand?"

"What if I don't want to know the truth?"

"Then, you will not be able to understand what is occurring. Then, you will not be able to prevent it from happening again, or if you do try to prevent it, you will be unable to do so effectively. Do you understand?"

"I don't know if I want to understand this."

"Chelsi, you have no choice. The truth will set you free. And it will set others free as well."

"Will it hurt?"

"It might."

"I don't want to know."

"Then you must choose ignorance."

Chelsi thought hard about what Abuela had said. She knew she had to do something. She had to do something for those poor souls whose lives were lost. She thought about the pain that she had felt after losing her parents. She thought about the guilt. She thought about the hopelessness.

She also thought about hope.

Hope is the only thing that keeps people alive, she decided. Hope is what kept her going. It was what got her out of bed every day. It was what made her want to live. It was what gave her the will to survive.

At last, Chelsi steeled herself and forced open her eyes. She looked out at the sea of people. "I must see this, Abuela," she whispered. Chelsi turned to see Abuela standing behind her.

"What's wrong? Are you okay? Did you see something that you don't want to remember?"

Chelsi shook her head.

"Good girl. Now, tell me what happened."

Chelsi recounted the entire experience to Abuela. She told her about the visions, the blood, the violence, and the dead slaves.

"Well, you have to let these things go, Chelsi. These things will haunt you forever if you hold on to them. Remember that you can't change the past. However, you can affect the future. You must learn from the past so that you may prevent similar atrocities from occurring in the future."

Chelsi wiped tears from her eyes. "Abuela, I just saw all of this. I saw it all. I felt it all!"

Abuela's face softened, and she cupped Chelsi's cheek with her hand.

"Oh, my dear, sweet girl. I know how you feel, but you mustn't think of it like that. You are not responsible for what has already occurred. You must focus on what you can do to prevent it from happening again. You must understand why this happened, and you must use your knowledge to prevent it from happening in the future."

"I wish I could talk to you about it."

"Of course, you can. That's what family is for."

"Thank you, Abuela."

The two sat quietly for a moment.

"Are you sure you're alright?" Abuela asked.

"Yeah, I'm fine."

"Did you see the future as well?"

"No, I didn't."

"Have you ever seen the future before?"

"No."

"What did you see?"

"A lot of dead slaves. A war. So much death!"

"Were there any other visions? Anything else that stood out?"

Chelsi thought for a moment.

"Other visions?"

"Yes, Chelsi! Other than the blood, and death, anything else you saw in the visions you aren't willing to share?"

"I just saw a whole bunch of people, Abuela."

"Do you mean African slaves?"

"Yeah," Chelsi said, nodding.

"And other people who were dead?"

"Yes."

Abuela put her head in her hands. She looked away as though she were trying to remember.

"Honestly, Abuela, I don't know."

"You didn't recognize them?"

"No, I didn't. There were so many people crowding around and yelling. I couldn't pay attention to any one person."

"Okay. Can you describe their clothing?"

"No. Their clothes were all different colors and styles. It was hard to tell what they wore."

"Did you find what you originally were looking for?" Abuela asked.

"No." Chelsi's shoulders slumped.

"What do you want to do mija?" asked her grandmother.

Chelsi looked up; she had a look of fierce determination that Alejandra hadn't seen on her granddaughter since she was a child.

"I'm going back in," Chelsi said.

They were about to start the ceremony again when they heard a loud banging on the door!

"Were you expecting company tonight?" Chelsi asked nervously.

"No," replied Abuela. They both looked at the front door for a long moment. Abuela walked over to the door, looked in the peephole, smirked and chuckled, then opened the door.

"Long time no see, Bruja," grunted a wet and battered Ronald Stanford.

***

CHAPTER 9

THE BEAST

Perhaps I should tell you a story about myself. About how I became what I am today. But first, I should warn you: you may not want to hear it.

You see, it has many, many sad parts. If you don't mind a bit of sadness, you might get a lot out of hearing it. So, sit back and enjoy the tale . . .

The main things I remember from childhood were hunger, thirst, and fear. All day long, every day, I lived with that constant, bone-deep terror that something horrible might happen to one or both of my parents at any moment.

England, 14ᵗʰ Century

When I was a child, I wasn't allowed to leave their side. I had to walk on eggshells around them, fearful that one misstep would result in punishment. They didn't have much love for us children—we were never allowed to play outside or even go into other rooms. We weren't really permitted to talk much, either. If we did, they punished us severely.

That included when I accidentally, (but loudly) called someone by his brother's name. His brother had died a while before, after falling off a roof. He'd been terribly hurt as a result. My father beat me when he heard what I said.

From that point on, my parents never allowed me to speak unless spoken to. That meant no talking at dinner, no answering questions, and no comments. Even whispering was forbidden. As soon as one of them gave a command, I had to obey immediately.

It was difficult for me to make friends because I couldn't interact with them in the way I wanted. I tried to keep it secret from them, but they caught me once and hit me so badly that I passed out and wound up with a huge bruise on my face. After that, I learned to stay quiet whenever possible.

Sometimes I thought they were punishing me because I was an accident. It seemed like they hated me and blamed me for everything wrong that happened.

To hide my feelings, I started acting out. First, it was small things—playing with my food, making faces, even sticking my tongue out at them. As I grew older, I started getting more and more dramatic. I began throwing tantrums if I didn't get my own way. I would scream and cry whenever they disciplined me.

In time, my parents stopped believing I was lying when I told them I'd done nothing wrong. That worsened things because they became more *harsh and crueler with me. The beatings got worse. Once, my mother even broke my arm.*

The worst part was the fear that something might happen to them. In my nightmares, I saw them die horribly right before me, and I was powerless to stop it.

One night, I woke up screaming from a terrible nightmare. When I looked over at my parent's bed, I found my dad lying beside my mom, dead. She hadn't moved at all.

It was too horrible to look at. I covered my eyes and buried my head under the pillow. After a few minutes, my mother stirred. She rolled over and opened her eyes.

"What's wrong?" she asked. "Are you all right?"

I shook my head. There was a sound in the hallway, and I recognized it instantly. It was a door opening and closing. Then another, and another. The footsteps sounded as if someone was walking down the hall, looking for us.

I could feel the blood pounding through my veins, my heart racing. I knew I had to hide, but I didn't know where I could go. I looked for a hiding place, somewhere out of sight. But there was nowhere to run.

There was a loud knock on the bedroom door, followed by my father's voice. "Open up!" he yelled. "We know you're in here."

My mother sat up and slowly stood, holding onto the edge of the bed. She walked toward the door, hesitating briefly before turning the knob and pushing it open.

She stepped into the hallway, her face pale. "What is it?" she whispered.

Before she could respond, I heard my father entering our room from behind her. "Where is she?" he demanded.

My mother turned around, looking startled to see him standing there. She blinked her eyes rapidly, as if trying to wake herself up.

He grabbed a fistful of her hair and yanked her backward. "I said, where is that devil spawn!?"

"I don't know," she answered.

He pushed her forward. "Didn't you hear me? Open the door!"

She took a step back, clutching at the doorknob. Her fingers slipped, and she fell to the ground, landing face-first on the floor.

For a moment, I was frozen, unable to move. My mother lay there on the floor, crying softly.

I wanted to help her, to comfort her somehow, but I didn't dare make a sound. Instead, I watched as my father kicked her in the stomach.

"Get up," he ordered. "Open the door."

My mother slowly stood up, tears streaming down her face. She reached out to touch the knob, then hesitated, shaking her head slightly.

Her father grabbed her by the neck and held her against his chest. "Don't you dare disobey me again, bitch." Then he pushed her toward the door and shoved her inside.

I waited until I heard the door close before I got up from the bed. I crept across the room and put my hand on my mother's shoulder. "Mom?"

She looked up at me. I could see the terror in her eyes.

"My child, I'm sorry," she whispered, "But I had to do it. For your sake. You have to understand."

I didn't answer. Instead, I just stared at her, feeling completely helpless.

Finally, she said, "He'll kill you if he finds out. I had to save you. Do you understand?" I nodded.

"Good," she said, squeezing my shoulders gently. Then she pulled away and straightened her clothes. "Now get dressed, my child. We have to leave."

She picked up my dirty clothes and handed them to me. I stood there without saying anything. After a moment, she sighed. "All right. If you won't, then maybe I will."

She ran her hands through my hair and kissed me on the forehead. "I love you, sweetheart. Don't you ever forget it."

Then she left the room, leaving me alone.

I stayed in that room for a long time. I didn't want to come out, to face the world, the outside, the people, the dangers. I felt safer inside the room with all its memories.

Eventually, though, I realized I couldn't stay there forever. I had to face reality, or else I would be trapped there for the rest of my life. I needed to get out. To escape.

And that's what I did.

I knew I had to leave that house and never return. I decided to run away. I packed a few changes of clothing and some food in a bag, then snuck out of the house one night.

I went to a nearby park and hid in a tree behind some bushes. I tried to sleep, but I kept seeing my parents' faces, hearing their voices, and watching them die.

I cried for hours. I didn't know what else to do.

At last, I fell asleep, exhausted from crying. I dreamed that I was being chased by my parents. They were coming after me, yelling at me to give back what I stole.

In my dream, I felt terrified. I ran as fast as I could, trying desperately to reach the safety of the trees.

But my parents were faster. They caught me easily, pinned me down, and began beating me again. This time, my mother was the one doing the hitting. She punched me several times in the stomach, then broke my arm.

They laughed as they did it, taunting me and threatening to kill me.

"Look at this, honey," my father said. "We've broken your arm. Now we can take it off. Maybe we'll keep it as a trophy."

I screamed and struggled, but they were too strong. They threw me to the ground and began kicking me.

It was the most horrible experience of my life. I woke up in a cold sweat, gasping for breath.

I stayed awake all night, waiting for morning. The next day, I finally got up and walked away. I had no idea where I was going, but I knew I had to find a new home.

I wandered the streets for days, searching for anyone who might help me. I asked strangers if they could spare any money. Most people ignored me or told me to go away, but a few of them gave me some coppers.

One man offered me a ride in his carriage, but when I refused, he threatened to call the militia. In those days, towns only had a formal police force much later in that era. Instead of a proper police force, a volunteer militia would be organized that sought to prevent small-scale theft and crime. Over time this militia of peasants would shift from a militia of volunteers to a permanently standing police force.

By the third day, I was tired and hungry. In fact, I had a fever, and I was beginning to shiver. It was starting to rain, which only made things worse. I was soaked and freezing.

On the fourth day, I collapsed and fell unconscious. I was lying on the ground beside a gutter when I woke up. It was dark outside, and I could barely move. I tried crawling forward, but I couldn't seem to make my muscles work.

Suddenly, I saw two men walking past me. One was wearing a hood that covered his face.

The other one was carrying a leather sack. He glanced down at me, then spat on the ground.

As they passed, the one in the hood kicked me hard in the ribs, knocking me to the ground. I tried to get up, but I was too weak. My legs wouldn't support me. I felt like a rag doll that someone had thrown aside.They left me there, on the ground, alone.

A couple of hours later, I heard a noise. Someone was coming toward me. A person! I hoped it was someone who could help me.

When I saw a woman approaching, I lifted my head and started to say something, but my mouth didn't seem to want to cooperate. I shook my head, trying to clear my thoughts.

"Hello?" she called out. "Can you talk?" I nodded, hoping she could see me.

"Okay, I'll be right back," she said. "Just stay there."

She disappeared quickly, and I wondered what was happening. A few minutes later, she returned, with a man following closely behind her.

"I hope you're feeling better," the woman said. She smiled at me. "My name is Dawn. What's yours?"

"I have no name," I croaked.

Dawn bent down and helped me sit up. When I looked at her, I noticed she was beautiful: long brown hair tied back in a ponytail, large blue eyes, and a soft smile.

"You're a beautiful child, aren't ya?" she said. "I'm so glad you came out of that heap of rubbish. Are you well?"

I laughed inwardly at the remark, for I was often mistaken for being younger than I actually was. I nodded, forcing myself to speak. "Do you think I could ask you a favor, please? Could you tell me how I can get to a shelter?"

"Of course," she answered. "What kind of shelter are you talking about?"

I explained to her what had happened to my family and how I'd been forced to run away. At first, she seemed shocked to hear everything, but then her expression softened. "Oh, honey," she said. "I'm so sorry. I wish I could help you. But I don't have any money to give you."

"All is well," I replied. "I don't need much. Just someplace to stay for the night."

"Well, what if I told you there was a shelter not far from here? Would that be good enough?"

I had to think about it for a minute. "Yes," I finally answered. "If there's a shelter nearby, I guess it would be fine."

"It is decided then!" Dawn smiled. "Let's get you there. Can you stand?"

I managed to get up and walk with her. As we headed toward the end of the block, I saw another man standing there.

"You!" he shouted. "This is private property! Get off the street, or I'll call the militia on ya!"

"Come on, my child," Dawn said. "We've already wasted enough time."

"But—" the man stammered.

Dawn turned and smiled at him. "Relax good sir. This sweet child is with me. She's safe with us." The man glared at me as if I were a criminal, but he didn't say anything.

We walked toward the corner, where Dawn led me down a side alleyway. The buildings along this stretch of the street were boarded up. There weren't any lights on inside them, and the windows were all covered with wooden shutters that hung loosely on their hinges.

The smell of sewage and decay filled the air. We walked for what felt like ages before we reached the place that Dawn had spoken of earlier. I saw the sign for it as soon as I turned the corner.

It was a small brick building just a few steps away from the sidewalk. The door was unlocked, and the woman who greeted us let us inside.

She showed Dawn to the kitchen while I sat on a metal bench at the front counter.

Only three other people were in the shelter — two men and a boy of teenage years. None of them paid any attention to me as I sat down.

I was still shaky from my ordeal, and it took me a moment to collect myself. Once I'd finished taking off my wet clothes in a place with some privacy, I wrapped myself in a blanket that hung on the wall. Then I curled up on the floor and tried to relax.

I kept thinking of my parents, wishing they had tried harder to love each other.

I thought of my childhood, playing in the yard with my dog. I remembered the happy times when I didn't have to worry about the perilous future.

I closed my eyes and tried to imagine a better future, one where I could live somewhere safe, where my mother had not abandoned me, where my father would not beat me to death in his anger.

For the rest of that night, I stayed awake. I kept thinking about what Dawn had told me about the shelter. I didn't know why she'd lied to me about it being close by or why she told me there was a room available for me.

I thought she did it because she cared about me. That meant she trusted me.

So, what did it mean? Did she really care about me? Or was she just pretending? Was she lying to make sure I'd stay there?

I tried to convince myself that it was probably the latter. After all, she appeared to be trying to help me. She wanted me to trust her, so I'd feel comfortable staying there. Still, I couldn't shake the feeling that there was more to it than that.

Around midnight, I found bucket and some water to wash my face. When I appeared in the kitchen the two men and the teenager were sitting in chairs around the dining table. Dawn was cooking something over the stove.

"Good evening," she said, smiling at me. "How are you feeling love?" I smiled back.

"I am as well as I can be, given the present circumstances," I said. "Thank you for helping me Miss."

She nodded. "It is not a problem. Right, let me warm you up some soup. You look cold." Before she could set the bowl in front of me, the teen grabbed it and started eating.

I stared at him for a moment. Then, without saying a word, I stood up and walked out of the room.

I went upstairs, looking for a place to sleep. My fever started returning, and there were no medicines available. Instead, I climbed into bed and pulled the covers over my body.

I lay there and stared at the ceiling, wondering what would happen next. I knew not when.

Sleep finally came near dawn, as invading thoughts of starting a new life, would only come from leaving here.

I woke up to the sound of someone screaming. I sat up in bed and listened as I tried to figure out where it was coming from.

Was it Dawn?

I jumped out of bed and ran downstairs.

When I opened the common room door, I discovered I was right. Dawn was on the floor, surrounded by a dozen angry men. Two of them held her wrists, while the others held her ankles. One of them was holding a knife.

"Stop this," I whispered. "Please, stop hurting her."

Nobody moved.

The other men stared at me, some laughing while others simply watched. I took a step closer to them. "Let her go," I demanded. "Now!"

They ignored me.

"Good sirs," I said, louder now. "She's scared, and she doesn't know what to do. Please, stop."

I saw Dawn shaking under the pressure of the men's hands. Her eyes were wide open, pleading with me to help her.

I stepped forward again, but suddenly, one of the men took a swing at me. He caught my shoulder and pushed me backward.

In the split second it took me to fall to the floor, the man with the knife lunged forward. He cut my arm before I could get up.

Blood gushed through my veins, spreading across my skin. I felt dizzy and lightheaded, like I couldn't breathe.

I tried to stand up, but the man with the knife shoved me back. Dawn screamed. She cried out for help.

"Stop this!" she yelled. "Stop it! Stop it!"

One of the men grabbed her by the hair and forced her to her knees. "Get off of her!" I screamed. "Don't hurt her anymore!"

The man holding the knife looked at me, then at Dawn. His eyes narrowed. "Who are you?" he asked. "Why are you interfering?"

I looked at Dawn, then back to him.

"I know not why you are doing this," I said. "But I won't allow you to hurt either of us."

The man laughed. "What makes you think you have any control over this situation?" he sneered. "Do you think you can beat us, welp? You're outnumbered, and you don't even have a weapon." The other men laughed, too. They began shouting abuse at me.

"You're nothing," one of them taunted. "Just another pathetic stray that this bitch picked up. You're useless."

I lowered my head. Tears streamed down my cheeks.

"Shut up!" the man with the knife said. "Enough of your games. This is between her and me. Now stand aside."

I stood up slowly. My leg was throbbing, and blood dripped onto the floor. I limped over to Dawn.

"Dawn," I said. "Be still, be still. Everything will be all right."

She shook her head, crying. "No. No, all IS NOT WELL! Lord save us!"

That is when the wolf came. To this day I know not why it chose that particular time to come to this abode. Perhaps it felt the heat and anger emanating from this sad dwelling. What I can say is that the event changed my life forever!

I saw it from the corner of my eye. I heard its howling cry as it ran out of the shadows and into the room.

It was huge, almost eight feet tall. Its fur was matted with mud and dirt, and it had dull, yellow eyes that glowed in the darkness.

The man with the knife spun around, his mouth open, ready to attack.

But the wolf was faster than he was. It leapt at him, knocking him off balance. Then, with a single swipe of its claws, it tore open his throat.

The man collapsed to the floor and stopped moving.

The wolf turned toward me. Its eyes were yellow and glowing. I backed away from it until I was pressed against the wall. I tried to run, but the wolf was faster than I expected.

Its paws knocked me down as it charged past me. It opened its jaws and snarled at me. "Run!" I screamed at Dawn. "Go get help!"

The wolf pounced on me; its teeth bared. I screamed as its claws dug into my chest. Blood flowed from my wounds, and I couldn't breathe.

Dawn screamed and ran toward the door; it turned and ran after her.

I struggled to my feet, watching helplessly as the wolf chased her down the stairs. I ran after it, stumbling down the hallway in the dark.

I tripped and fell to my hands and knees. I crawled toward Dawn, following the trail of blood. I found her on the ground. She was still alive but barely breathing.

I lifted her up in my arms. She opened her eyes, and I could see that she was terrified. "Where are we?" she asked me.

The sound echoed off the walls, growing louder with every passing minute. The house became filled with smoke, akin to the fires of hell and I could feel the heat rising from the flames!

A bullet hit the floor beside me "Get out of here," a voice whispered. I spun around. A shadow stood there, looking at me with cold, dead eyes. He held a gun in his right hand.

He fired another shot at the creature chasing them. It missed and disappeared through a hole in the wall.

Then he fired again. This time the bullet hit the beast, and it yelped in pain!

But it wasn't enough. The beast lunged forward, grabbing him by the throat! He let go of the gun and tried to pull the wolf's paw from his neck. But the wolf squeezed tighter.

Finally, the man let go of the wolf's paw and grabbed the barrel of the gun. The wolf lunged forward, trying to bite the man. He pulled the trigger. I heard the gunshot and then felt a sharp pain in my shoulder.

I looked back and saw the man lying on the ground, clutching his arm.

The wolf was on top of him now, its jaws open wide. It was going to kill him.

I screamed for It to stop, but It didn't listen.

I picked up the gun and aimed it at the wolf. I squeezed the trigger.The weapon clicked.

No, I thought. I don't want to die like this!

Then the wolf let go of the man. It turned toward me. Its eyes were burning with anger.

It reached toward me. I turned my head to avoid the attack.

The wolf bit my arm, tearing skin and flesh along the way. Blood poured from the wounds.

I stumbled backward, falling onto the stairs. The wolf jumped over the body of the man who tried to help me.

Dawn was gone.

I could hear fire raging outside. The flames were getting closer. I turned around and noticed the broken window. The wolf leapt through the opening. It landed on the lawn.

I followed, crawling on all fours across the grass and dirt. I got to my feet and ran into the woods. The buildings were ablaze with orange light.

There was nobody in sight.

I looked back at the house. Flames flickered inside, casting strange shapes onto the walls. Thick black smoke billowed out of the front door.

I turned around and hurried away from the burning building. I returned to the shelter later that morning.

My head was pounding, and I was exhausted from the previous night's events.

I know something in me was changed. I could see more, smell more, and FEEL MORE! But I needed to figure out what or how, and I wasn't sure if it would last.

Dawn and the others were gone. Their clothes had been piled in the corner of the room, along with their blankets. There were signs of a struggle.

The front door was unlocked, and I walked outside.

I didn't have the energy to search for them. All I wanted to do was lie down and rest.

I sat down on one of the benches nearby and closed my eyes. As I drifted into sleep, I could hear a faint voice whispering in my ears.

"Come to me, child, you're of my pack now!" said the wolf.

I woke up with a jolt. The sun was shining brightly overhead, and it was late afternoon. I took a deep breath. The wolf was gone.

That night, I slept through dinner. When I woke up in the morning, I checked my arm and chest. The bleeding had stopped, and the wounds were healing.

I went downstairs and ate breakfast alone. Afterward, I went upstairs to one of the bedrooms, laid down on the bed, and closed my eyes.

I could feel the wolf in my mind, waiting for me to join him, could sense his presence in the darkness and thought about him for a long time.

I knew that I shouldn't talk to him, but I couldn't help myself. "I'm tired of running," I said to him. "I'm tired of being afraid." I waited for him to reply, but he didn't answer.

I stayed there for hours, thinking about him. Eventually, I felt his presence fade away.

I opened my eyes and got up.

I put on my coat and headed for the door. I didn't really know where I was going. I just needed to walk. To clear my thoughts.

I spent the next few days walking around town aimlessly, and have been walking around towns aimlessly ever since.

I have met many others of my kind over the centuries, but I have never felt the inclination to engage them, unless they could offer me service. Most of the wolves I've met are like me: solitary. We don't have much choice if we want to survive. There is no pack for us to belong to, no place where we can be safe. We live our lives as lone wolves, in Adam's paradise.

CHAPTER 10

LITTLE HAVANA
ABUELA'S APARTMENT, EVENING

"What are you doing here, and what happened to you?" Abuela asked.

"I'll tell you everything that went down if you let me in. Please make a decision fast; the cops are probably looking for me; I left behind a big mess," Ronald said.

Abuela stared at him with her stern face. "Okay, but first, I need to know that my granddaughter is not in danger."

"Granddaughter? You have a granddaughter?!"

"Yes, and she's inside," Abuela said.

Ronald opened the door slowly. He looked around the hallway before entering. When he was sure it was clear, he walked into the room. Abuela looked at him quizzically. "Who did you think was in here?" She asked.

"Old habits," Ronald said. Abuela led him to the back room. What he saw gave him chills, though he had been in this room before. He would never forget this place as long as he lived. It was the exact same room as the one on the night he'd visited Abuela years ago. He had needed her help to escape something. It is what had driven him out of the Agency and almost led him to suicide by alcohol.

But that was another story.

On the opposite side of the room from Abuela sat an attractive, younger woman; Ronald realized he may have just come in the middle of something. This must be the granddaughter the Bruja had been talking about, he thought. She looked like she could use some help. "Can you tell me who you are? "Ronald asked.

"Don't worry, I won't say anything," the young woman said. Her face was pale and shivering uncontrollably despite the room's heat.

"Are you okay?"

"I'm fine," she replied.

"No, really, are you okay?"

"Of course, I am. Don't worry, I've got this," Chelsi said confidently. Then she looked over at Abuela. "Please, we have to talk."

"I'm right here my love," Abuela said. "Why don't you introduce yourself to our guest."

The young woman looked up at Ronald, then back at Abuela. "Hello, my name is Chelsi, nice to meet you. Then she looked appraisingly at Ronald. "What the hell happened to you?" she asked incredulously, you look like someone threw you in the washing machine!"

Ronald tried not to show it, but he was shaken by the remark. He didn't know where to begin explaining himself. "I'm sorry, I . . ."

"Normally I would be more patient, but I have had a really bad night. You couldn't have come at a worse time. So, for the sake of brevity, just spit it out!" She demanded.

"Alright . . . okay. Just calm down, okay? First, let me explain why I'm here; then we can go from there."

Chelsi sat quietly and listened intently as he explained everything that had happened since last night. "So . . . you're telling me that someone or something took out all the guards and the man that hired you all by itself, and you can't tell me what it looks like?" Chelsi asked. "What kind of private security guard are you?"

She was being sarcastic, but Ronald didn't take offense. "Look, I'm sure you're a nice girl, but you're going to have to trust me on this. I've seen more than enough strange things in my life to believe this is real. Now, I'm afraid I have to leave. If anyone finds me here, they'll assume I killed everyone. It may have been a bad idea to come here, but I didn't know where else to go."

"Wait, wait, wait!" Chelsi said. "Where are you going?"

"I've gotta figure out how to get out of town now that the job is done, and the cops are on my tail. It's not safe here anymore. Like

I said, I never should have come here. Since we are playing twenty questions, what were you and the Bruja up to before I darkened your door?"

Chelsi looked at Abuela, then back to Ronald. "We were trying to find out why I've been having recurring nightmares about some creature with gold eyes," she said. "It happens every time I go to bed, and it has been happening more often. It feels like I'm being watched during the dreams."

"You think this thing is watching you?"

"Yeah, pretty much."

"And you can't remember anything else about the dream?"

"Nothing except the feeling that something bad is going to happen." She paused, thinking about what she wanted to say next. "Something dark is coming."

Ronald looked blankly at her. "Did you say yellow eyes?" he asked.

"Yellow eyes . . . and claws," she replied. "Why are you asking?"

"Because whatever threw me into the pool had yellow eyes," Ronald said.

"So, what does this mean? We both saw the same thing, but it still may mean nothing, or even may be some crazy coincidence."

"If those two things are connected, it might be important to compare notes."

"Like what notes?"

"I don't know yet."

Chelsi sighed in frustration. "Well, I guess I'll see you later then," she said. Before Ronald could respond, she turned around and started walking towards the front door.

"Chelsi, wait!" Ronald called after her. "Listen, I'm sorry for what I said to you earlier."

"I know you are, but I don't have the energy for it right now. I'm leaving, and I'll see you later if I even see you again, good luck with the cops."

"You don't want to try again?" Abuela asked. Chelsi stopped walking.

She turned around and faced them, her hands balled into fists. "I'm not taking any more chances with that thing out there."

Abuela nodded. "That's fair. But you should know that we are getting closer to finding out who is responsible for all this."

Abuela turned to Ronald. "My granddaughter told me that she has been having nightmares for months and that they have been getting worse recently. If there is some sort of connection between her nightmares and what happened to you yesterday, we should try to find out. Maybe if we knew the cause, we would know how to stop whoever or whatever is killing these people."

"I'm not sure I want to know what's causing these nightmares," Chelsi said. "I don't care if it is just a coincidence; I'll deal with the nightmares as long as they stay just nightmares. I don't know how many times I can handle seeing something like what a saw earlier tonight. We gave it our best, but maybe we should quit while we're ahead." She closed her eyes and shook her head as though trying to shake the memory off.

"Mija, I understand how you feel, but this isn't just going to go away. Just give us a chance to find out what's going on, alright?" Abuela said.

Chelsi sighed in relief. "All right, I will. But if I end up going crazy, I will not be responsible for what happens."

It took everything Chelsi had left to make her way back into that back room. Ronald was going to follow her, but Abuela put a hand on his chest. "Stay here," she whispered.

"But—"

She shook her head and gave him an encouraging smile. He didn't move, so she spoke louder: "I'll be right back."

He nodded as though he understood, then turned to watch through the open door.

Chelsi made it three steps into the back room before the tears fell. She sat near the altar for a long time, staring down at her hands, until they started shaking. Her face felt hot; her body ached from the tightness in her chest. She ran a hand over her cheek, wiping away the tears that were already making tracks on her skin. This couldn't go on forever, could it?

The room smelled like incense and meat. Not bad, but somehow off-putting. Chelsi tried to stay focused—her mother's voice echoed in her ears, always repeating how important it was to keep your thoughts clear.

Her grandmother put a hand on her shoulder. "You must find the strength inside to do this; this evil will not go away," Abuela said fiercely.

"Grandma—"

"Do you know why I came to America?" Abuela asked.

Chelsi shook her head.

"Because it is a land of opportunity!" Abuela said with great passion.

"We have worked hard to build our home here, and now you, the next generation, must work harder than ever."

"I don't understand."

Her grandmother held up a finger. "This is an important lesson. You must let nothing distract you from your purpose. Do not give anyone else power over you. Only by becoming strong enough to stand against those who would hurt us can we protect our family, protect the innocent!"

Her grandmother's words seemed to carry more weight when she looked into Chesli's eyes. There was something in them that Chelsi could feel deep within herself. Abuela continued. "We are taught that no one else will lift us up if we fall. That is why we must help each other rise."

"But what about . . . " Chelsi began, but Abuela cut her off with a wave of her hand.

"There is no more time for debate. Our enemies are coming, and they will do anything in their power to destroy us." Abuela drew in a breath. "You will learn the ways of your new life soon enough, but first, you must deal with this. The spirit world is very real. It is where we go when we die or wish to communicate with our ancestors. You are not alone in this!"

Chelsi nodded, "Let's do this." They both sat back down in the positions they were in earlier.

"Calm your mind," Abuela said. "Let the spirit guide you to where you need to go!"

Chelsi felt her body relax; her breath steady. She closed her eyes and pulled the pain from her heart, letting it slip out with the tears that followed.

Just before she opened her eyes again, she saw a shape appear between the pillars of the shrine on the opposite side of the altar. It was tall and thin, with long hair that hung around its shoulders. In its left hand, it held a sword of blue fire.

"Who are you?" she whispered, her voice quivering.

The spirit reached out toward Chelsi with a pale hand as though trying to touch her. Chelsi moved closer to the altar, not wanting to get too far from her grandmother, afraid she might vanish if she wasn't careful. The spirit stepped forward, then suddenly, the world seemed to swirl around her. She stumbled backward, almost falling.

"Chelsi! Chelsi!" Abuela called, reaching for her.

In the distance, she heard a woman screaming. Then there was a thump like someone had dropped a heavy book.

She was in the clouds flying above Miami, above everything. She could see the entire city in its full splendor. The lights reflected off the ocean. Palm trees waved in the breeze.

"Is this a dream?" she asked.

A figure appeared beside her. She recognized her instantly. It was her mother. "Yes, Chelsi."

Chelsi was overcome with emotion. "Mama!"

Her mother smiled at her. There were tears in her eyes and they were so happy to see each other like that. They embraced tightly, crying into each other's shoulders. Her mother had always been the most beautiful woman inside and out.

Chelsi pulled away from her mom just long enough to look down at the city below them. "I can't believe it's real," she said, awestruck by what lay before her.

"It is," her mother replied. "And you are home."

"What does this mean?"

"That you're finally ready to learn."

She looked out over the city, seeing it from a different perspective. As she did, she realized that it was the same view as the one outside the window of the plane.

Something was wrong. She could sense it, but she couldn't explain why.

When she looked back at her father, he was gone, replaced by the spirit again. This time it didn't reach for her but stood in front of her.

"Your mother is dead, Chelsi," it said. And your father is lost. If you survive, he will need you now more than ever.

"But . . . I'm not dead. I am still alive."

"No, you are not," the spirit replied. "You are not alive. And you are not dead."

"How can I be both alive and dead?"

You are something else. Something greater."

"Greater than what?"

The spirit smiled and pointed to the city below. "Look."

She stared down, trying to make out what she was looking at. It was too far away, and the moon was in her eyes.

Suddenly, she saw it. People were walking along the streets, moving like ants.

"What is that?" she asked.

"They are the living. The dead walk amongst them, and they do not even notice."

Chelsi shook her head. "This isn't possible."

The spirit laughed. "Of course, it is. Everything is possible. But you are not meant to understand this yet. You must focus on the task at hand and remember your goal. Nothing else matters. Your parents are gone, but that doesn't matter. What matters is protecting others from the enemy."

"What enemy?"

"All of them. All your enemies. Everyone and everything that wishes harm upon you and your people."

"Why would anyone want to harm me?"

"Because they hate you, and they fear you."

Chelsi considered what the spirit said, then asked. "Why would they be afraid of me?"

"Because you are not of this world, and they know this."

"So, I should hide, just like my parents hid?"

"Sometimes it is necessary to fight. To stand and defend yourself. If you don't, you will never survive."

Chelsi looked up again. "If I am not meant to understand, how will I ever do this?"

"You will learn the rest of the lessons as you need them. Just remember that what you are doing is necessary. You must act like your ancestors before you but be part of the future. Find the Red Wolf!"

The spirit faded away, leaving Chelsi alone in the clouds.

She looked down at Miami once more. The city was so beautiful, yet people were moving through it as if they weren't even aware of the beauty around them. She knew that they were hiding from something, but she didn't know what.

She concentrated, straining to hear any sound that might be coming from below. After a few minutes of silence, she decided to try another approach. Instead of listening, she watched.

People walked into traffic and got hit by cars. Others ran across the street without looking. A man yelled at a police officer, but the cop didn't respond.

Chelsi couldn't understand why anyone would do these things. They all seemed so careless.

Perhaps they were scared. Or maybe she was missing something important.

As she focused on the city, she began to see something strange. Her eyes were drawn to the sky, following the movement of the people below. She couldn't stop watching. For the first time, she noticed patterns in their movements. She began to watch carefully, trying to find some clue about what was happening.

After a while, she became convinced that something was going on. She strained to listen but heard nothing except for the noise of traffic and voices. She looked around the clouds, but there was no sign of the spirit.

Then she felt the pull.

She focused on the pull of frenzied primal madness. Everything around her turned black, but she could still feel its power.

Suddenly a vision coalesced in front of her. She could tell something was sleeping, but there was no form or shape to it. Then the image sharpened, and the evil's eyes opened. The yellow and golden eyes twinkled with entertainment!

**"NIIIICEEEE TOOOOO MEEETT YOOUUU . . .
CHELSIIIIIIIIIIIIII!!!" I"LL SEEEEE YOUUU SOON!!**

The voice echoed in her mind, and Chelsi began to panic. She was still connected, but she could barely hear it.

She tried to scream, but no sounds came. She tried to move, but her muscles wouldn't obey her.

And she was trapped, unable to escape.

She screamed in her mind, "Help!"

She wanted so desperately to cry. But no tears would come. She felt terrible pain, like an invisible knife was being driven into her spine.

"Please someone help!" she cried out.

No one answered. No one cared. The vision ended, and Chelsi collapsed on the floor at the altar, trembling uncontrollably. Her legs were weak, and she could hardly breathe.

"Chelsi, are you okay?" Abuela asked.

Chelsi nodded and started crying. She didn't know why, but she was overwhelmed with emotion. It was all she could do just to hold herself up.

"What happened?" Abuela asked.

Chelsi said between sobs. "It was horrible."

Chelsi spent the next hour curled up on the altar, crying and holding her grandmother. Abuela rubbed her back, trying to comfort her.

When she finally calmed down, she told Abuela what had happened.

"I'm so sorry, Chelsi," her grandmother said. "Maybe we should leave."

Abuela was right. Chelsi hadn't been able to cope with a spirit; she'd never imagined that she might encounter something like this. It made her wonder what else she was capable of.

"I don't think so," Chelsi said. "I'm here to stay until we've learned the way of the spirits."

"But what if you can't handle this? I don't know what happened but pushing yourself right now seems like a bad idea, you need rest first."

"I'll be okay," Chelsi said. "As long as we stick together."

"I'm sure we will, always. But I fear for you, by pushing you, I have put you in danger."

"I'm not in danger, Grandma. I am danger! Like you said, I can't play it safe forever."

Abuela smiled. "You'll find that most warriors aren't very good at being safe. It's much easier to fall into trouble than it is to avoid it, I'm afraid."

"I know," Chelsi said. "I don't plan on staying home and waiting for this thing to come get me. We have to go out and look for it."

"And you think you can find it?"

"I hope so."

"I'm sure you will."

***

CHAPTER 11

LITTLE HAVANA
ABUELA'S APARTMENT, EVENING

Ronald tried to think of his next move as he threw his clothes into the dryer. Abuela gave him some clothes to try on that her son-in-law had left there years ago; they fit well enough.

He went to the bathroom to take a quick shower and change into his new outfit. Abuela had provided him with a medical kit to bandage the wound he received at the hands of that . . . thing. It was not nearly as bad as it could have been, but it would need some time to heal. He didn't want to risk infection.

Luckily, there weren't that many people out and about when he escaped the crime scene at the resort earlier, so he didn't have to explain the blood on his forearm. Before his present occupation, Ronald had made living at being a ghost, to effortlessly blend into his environment. He had walked out of more than one mission bloody, Ronald made sure to tuck his gun into his pants' waistband, so he could grab it quickly if he needed to. He had gotten rid of his phone hours ago, taking out the SIM card and destroying the phone.

He was glad that he had done that. At least now, he wouldn't have to worry about being tracked or traced.

Another pair of shoes wasn't available, so he would have to walk around barefoot until they dried; he was going nowhere for a while.

He walked down the hall and knocked on the door to Chelsi's room.

"Come in," came a muffled reply from inside.

He opened the door and peeked inside. Chelsi was sitting up in bed, staring at the ceiling.

"Hey," Ronald said.

"Hi, Ron," she said.

"How are you feeling?"

She shrugged. "Okay, I have a lot to think about."

"What to talk about it?"

"Not right now. I'm fine, really."

"I'm sure you are, but you shouldn't push yourself."

"I'm not, but thanks for looking out for me," Chelsi insisted. "I guess you're actually not a bad guy."

"Thanks, I think." Ronald replied. "You don't need to be stubborn about this. If you don't feel better tomorrow, then come talk to me."

"I might take you up on that," she said. "But right now, I'm okay."

Ronald smiled. "Good, get some sleep, we are probably going to need it in the days to come."

He stepped out of the room and closed the door behind him. As he headed down the hall, he took a deep breath. This was probably his last day in Miami. That was okay with him, but it was also depressing. He thought about calling his family but decided against it. His mother would only worry; he didn't want to put them through that. He had already caused enough trouble tonight.

Besides, he had to get moving soon.

He had to figure out where he should go next. He couldn't go home, not until all of this blew over, but he didn't know where else to go. The Agency was bound to get wind of his troubles with the law anytime now. He wouldn't be surprised if there were agents casing his place right now! He never for one second assumed that the Agency would ever stop keeping tabs on him. He knew too much, had done too much.

There were many places he could probably go—places to hide and lie low for a while. Maybe somewhere in South America. But that wasn't his goal. He didn't want to disappear forever. He had to clear his name.

That meant finding the bastard that killed his team before someone else did.

***

Chelsi woke up the next morning feeling somewhat refreshed. She stood and stretched, running her hands down her body to ensure she was okay. She felt perfectly normal, though her head still hurt. She sat back down, relieved that the spirit hadn't visited her during the night.

Abuela was still asleep in the other room, so she lay down on top of the covers and went back to sleep. She was starving when she woke up again, so she dressed and went downstairs for breakfast.

Abuela was already at the table, eating a bowl of cereal. She was wearing her usual loose-fitting dress, and her hair was pulled back in a ponytail. She smiled when she saw Chelsi walking toward her.

"Good morning, Chelsi," she said. "Did you sleep well?"

"Yeah, I guess, as well as could be expected."

"It's good that you're feeling better," Abuela said. "I'm sorry that the spirit bothered you last night. I'll try to warn you next time. Would you like some coffee?"

"Sure."

Abuela poured two cups of black coffee and handed one to Chelsi.

"Thanks."

She drank the coffee, and it tasted great, then took a bite of her toast and chewed slowly.

"Do you think we should go look for this wolf?" Chelsi asked after she finished chewing. She was all in last night, but after a good night's sleep and time to think about what they were ACTUALLY going to attempt, Chelsi found that she was falling back into a mindset of retreat.

"Yes, I believe that we should." Abuela replied. "So far, you haven't been able to sense its location. If it was closer to you, you might be able to pick up its energy."

"I was afraid you were going to say that," Chelsi said.

"You want to go today?" Abuela asked.

"I don't know. I'd like to, but I don't know if I'm ready yet. What do you think?"

"If you feel up to it, then yes. I can help you. But if you need more rest, or if your headache comes back, then we won't go."

"I'll be okay," Chelsi said. "I don't think it's going to come back. I think I'm ready."

She finished the toast and poured herself a second cup of coffee.

Abuela smiled and sipped her coffee.

Ronald entered the kitchen; he didn't look like he hadn't slept well. Chelsi felt for him; until now, he was the only one who had physically seen what they were going up against. He had seen the Beast, and he knew how powerful it was.

"Morning," he said. "How are you feeling?"

"Better," Chelsi said. "I've decided to go look for that thing, but I don't know where to start."

"Why don't you let me come with you, I have some experience hunting people." Ronald asked.

Chelsi was interested. She wanted to ask what he did for a living that involved hunting people, but she decided to table that question for another time. Instead, she said. "No, it's okay," Chelsi said. "I can handle this myself."

Ronald looked at her skeptically. "What's the plan?"

Chelsi looked at him. "I don't have one, but I'll work one out as I go along."

He nodded and turned back toward the door.

"You can stay here if you want," she said. He shook his head. She followed him out into the hall.

"Where are we going?" he asked.

"I've got a feeling that whatever happened last night was not just a coincidence, "Chelsi continued. "And even if it was a coincidence and all this could be simply fixed with some therapy and a couple of Ambien, how would that explain why you were here?"

Ronald thought about it for a moment. Then he shrugged his shoulders. "I don't know. Maybe I'm just crazy or something."

They stood there for a minute, unsure where they were going next. Chelsi had always been bad at making decisions. It seemed that as soon as she made up her mind about something, or someone, something else came along to change it. Now she wondered if she had made the right choice. If this was just a dream, she didn't need to worry about it anymore. But she knew better. There was no way that everything that had happened were just hallucinations. She still had to figure out how this vison thing worked. Though her grandmother had given her the support and confidence to delve into the void and acknowledge the Beast's existence, she still could not sense WHERE it was. Her grandmother's powers were no help either. Abuela explained that her powers worked differently than Chelsi's. She needed a subject's possession to divine information on them.

"I think I know someone who may be able to help you." Abuela added. "He is an old friend, though we haven't talked due to a disagreement we had years ago over his occupation. This is not the first time I have dealt with the creatures of the night. In the old country, there were men and women raised and trained to hunt these creatures. They are called the Vigilantes Nocturnos, or Night Watchmen. Some even call them the "Night Guard," but most people just refer to them by their nickname: The Nocturnal." They worked for centuries with Bruja to keep villages safe from supernatural creatures. They are skilled in all manners of weapons, lure and hand, to hand combat."

Chelsi wasn't sure what to say. She wanted to thank her Grandmother for helping her find a solution. She also didn't want to get involved with some sort of vigilante group, but at this point, her options were limited. What choice did she really have?

"Thank you so much, Abuela. That may be just what we need to turn the tide!" She said excitedly.

"Don't thank me yet, child. I am not certain he will agree to help, and even if he does, there is a great risk. He works alone now, and I'm afraid he has become quite reclusive. He once told me that he doesn't like having people around him. He lives in Homestead, where there are more isolated places to live. He reminds me of you, a little. Isn't that why you moved away from Miami? To get away from people?" Abuela asked.

Chelsi laughed, "Yeah, it was." She paused for a moment, thinking. "But if he can help me, I'll make an exception." She looked over to Ronald. "Let's take my car, the cops are probably looking for yours."

"Then it is settled," said Abuela. I will call him now. Start heading to Homestead, hopefully, he will give you a warm welcome.

"Sure thing," Chelsi replied.

She turned back to Ronald. "Hey, I'm sorry. About before."

Ronald shook his head. "It's alright. I've learned to expect that from crazy women," he said jokingly.

Chelsi smiled. At least he wasn't mad at her anymore. "Well, I guess I deserved that," she said sheepishly.

He shrugged. "For what it's worth, I don't think you're crazy. I think you're a very brave woman, and I hope I don't disappoint you."

Chelsi looked down, surprised. She hadn't thought anyone would ever feel that way about her. She was touched, and embarrassed that she had let herself cry after he left.

"Good luck," Abuela said.

***

CHAPTER 12

HOMESTEAD, FLORIDA, AFTERNOON

The drive to Homestead was uneventful.

Abuela had phoned ahead and arranged for a meeting with Alfred Delecruz, one of the Watchmen, at his place on the outskirts of the town. When they arrived, they thought their GPS had taken them to an abandoned meth house. A dilapidated two-story house sat beside a field of weeds. There were no signs of life anywhere.

To the right of the house, the largest tree they had ever seen this far south, stretched its branches over a fence and blocked the road. It was the only other visible landmark besides the house itself.

"This doesn't look like the kind of place you'd come to ask for help," Chelsi commented. "This looks like the place you would get hunted down by inbred hillbillies like in the movies!"

"We can't judge a book by its cover. Sometimes the best things hide in plain sight," Ronald said.

Chelsi nodded and parked the car beside the old house. "Is anybody home?" she asked. Her voice sounded weak and scared.

Nothing.

She exited her car, took another step forward, and a large black bird flew out from under the tree. It flapped its wings and landed on the ground next to her.

"Are you with him?" Chelsi asked.

The bird looked at Chelsi and cawed.

"Is that you talking?" Chelsi asked.

The bird hopped up onto the branch above Chelsi's head and fluttered its wings a few times.

"Thank you," Chelsi said.

"You're welcome," Alfredo Delacruz said.

Chelsi felt her heart almost come out of her chest! She didn't even notice that Ronald was out of the car, with his hand at the small of her back.

"That will not be necessary," Delacruz said. Despite the deadpan look on his face, his eyes looked amused at the whole affair.

Alfredo Delacruz was an impressive-looking older man. He had thick black hair, and a prominent beard that was neatly trimmed. His skin was dark. It looked like he spent some time outdoors in the sun when he grew up. He had intense green eyes that looked like they could see through any lie you attempted to tell. When he smiled, his teeth were very white against his dark skin.

"Hello," he said with a smile. "I'm Alfredo Delacruz."

He offered his hand to shake. Chelsi shook it and introduced herself.

"Nice to meet you," he replied. "So, do you want to come inside?"

"Yes that would be great," Chelsi said. "This my friend, Ron, can he come with me?"

"Only if he promises not to fire his weapon at anything in the house,"

The inside of the house was nice enough. It was small, but it looked like it would be easy to keep clean. The kitchen was tiny, but there were two dining tables in the living room for larger groups. There were three bedrooms on the second floor, and one seemed to have been converted into an office or study.

As soon as they entered, Chelsi noticed a few pictures on the walls. One was of another family photo; she assumed this was his wife and kids. When they were in the house, she reintroduced Ronald to Alfredo. They had agreed to let her do all of the talking on the drive here.

"You can grab something to drink if you lik," Alfredo offered. "I don't get many visitors here."

They took their drinks into the living room, where they found him sitting down at a table with a book open in front of him. They sat across from each other.

"So, what brings you all the way out here?" Alfredo asked her after we'd taken a sip of our drinks.

Chelsi started from the beginning. She told him about the visions and her suspicion that a real monster was out there hunting people. When she was done, Delecruz was looking at her speculatively. He began asking her questions, trying to find out how much she really knew.

When she finished, he was quiet. Then he reached over the bar and poured himself a glass of rum. He downed it in one go, then went back to staring at Chelsi. She tried to figure out what he was thinking.

Then he stood up, walked around the table, and set his glass down. 'Let's go outside," he said.

She followed him out onto the porch. He motioned for her to sit on the couch, which she did. She didn't know why he wanted to talk out there.

After a moment, he turned to face her. "'Do you believe in monsters?" he asked.

She looked at him questioningly, wondering if she should tell him everything. After a moment, she decided to trust him. "Yes." She said simply.

Delacruz nodded. "Good." Then he leaned forward and put his hand on hers. They were still sitting down, but his fingers were long and thin compared to hers. He ran his hand over them slowly as if searching for something. "Tell me about your dreams."

She did. She described the first dream she ever had. Then she talked about the others until she was finished.

After that, he sat silently for several minutes. Then he stood up and walked into the house.

Chelsi waited a moment, then followed him inside. He was standing by the bar, staring into space.

He turned to her. "What was the last thing you saw in your vision?" He asked.

It had been bothering her since she woke up. What was the last thing she saw? She thought it over, realizing it was the creature's shadow. So, she told him, 'It was the monster.'

He nodded. "How does it move?" he asked.

She frowned. "'I don't know," she said. "I couldn't see it clearly. It just came out of nowhere. That's the part that bothers me the most. I mean, I know it was a dream, but I felt like I was really awake."

He nodded again. "'Did it have any characteristics?" he asked.

She hesitated. "Well, it was large and dark and covered in fur. But beyond that, I couldn't say."

Delacruz nodded again. "Thank you. Do you think it has anything to do with the killings that have been on the news?"

She shrugged. "Probably," she admitted. "But I don't know. I wish I knew more about it. I just hope you can help."

He smiled. "We'll start there then," he said simply. "Come on, let's go outside."

They walked out onto the porch and sat down once again. "There are a few things you should know before we begin," he told her. "First, I can't guarantee that this will work. Even if you're right, and this is a monster, there is no guarantee that we can catch it. And even if we do, it might not stop killing people."

She frowned. "'I understand," she said. "But I feel like I'm doing something. If nothing else, I can try to warn people."

He nodded. "There's a chance that if we find this thing, we can stop it from killing anyone else. However, that doesn't mean we won't fail. You need to be prepared for either outcome. Are you ready?"

She sighed, "I guess so. What do you want me to do now?"

He gestured to the book he'd been reading. "'Have you ever heard of the legend of the El Lobizon?"

She shook her head. "No."

He opened the book and flipped through a few pages. "There are two different versions of this story," he explained as he read. "One version says that a creature known as the Lobizon was responsible for the deaths of thousands of people. The other says that it was an old man who lived alone in the forest. He had the power to turn into a wolf."

Chelsi listened intently. If this was true, then it meant that Chelsi was right. This was the creature she was seeing in her dreams.

He continued reading the legend. In both versions, the Lobizon killed men, women, and children. It made its home in the woods but never left the area. People were warned to stay away from it. None of them did, and the monster destroyed them.

It continued killing over the years until, eventually, there was no one left alive. Then, it disappeared. It had probably died or moved on. Whatever the case, the stories stopped after that.

That was the end of the book.

He closed it, then looked at her. 'What do you think?' he asked.

She thought it sounded like the same thing she saw in her dreams. "It sounds exactly the way my nightmares always end," she told him.

He nodded. "Then let's start looking. But before we do, there are a few things I need to make sure you understand."

"What do you mean?' she asked.

"Well, first of all, we need to be careful. These creatures aren't human. They're monsters, and it's possible they've developed ways of hiding their presence from us. We'll have to be smart and pay attention to what we see.

"Second, I can't promise that this will work. There's a chance that we'll spend the next few months tracking this creature, only to find out that it's not out there. That means you could be wasting your time and maybe even putting yourself in danger. Are you okay with that?"

"I guess so," she said hesitantly.

"Okay, good. Let's move on to the fun stuff," he announced. "This is going to be dangerous. It's possible you might get hurt or worse. Are you willing to do whatever it takes to find this creature? Even if it means risking your life?"

She took a breath. "I don't know," she finally said. "What happens if I agree to this, and we discover that this isn't the creature we're looking for?"

"Then you lose nothing," he answered simply. "Besides, it's better than just waiting around for it to kill someone else."

"Okay, I'm in. Where do we start?" she asked.

"First, we need to learn more about these creatures," he said. "So we need to start with the books. We'll go through every single one of them and see what we can learn. Once we've learned enough, then we'll move on to our next step."

He turned to leave. "Wait!" Chelsi called out. "What about my dreams?"

He paused. "Those are important too," he noted. "They could be valuable to our investigation."

"Okay," she agreed. "Can you tell me what they mean, though? Is there any significance to them? Aren't they supposed to be warnings?"

"That's what they used to be," he explained. "But it appears that things have changed. Now, your dreams may actually be showing you something important. This means that if we can figure out what that something is, we have a shot at catching this thing. Is that important to you?" he asked.

"Yes," she said without hesitation.

"All right let's get started then," he said and headed off into the house.

Chelsi followed behind him. She walked into the kitchen, and Alfredo opened a cabinet. He pulled out a small box of tea bags and handed it to her. 'You can use this to brew the teas,' he explained. "Just give me one cup of water from the tap in the bathroom, and I'll have it ready when you're done."

She nodded and followed him back to the living room. He pointed to the couch, and she sat down. He sat across from her, picked up the book, and began flipping through it.

"These are all the books I have that deal with paranormal creatures," he explained. "There are hundreds of them. Some of them are fiction, others are historical accounts, and some are just plain weird. All of them come from all over the world."

She nodded as she looked through the titles. A few were familiar, but most were completely unknown to her. It would take her weeks to go through them all.

"I'll start with these," he said, pointing to the first few on the top shelf. He grabbed a handful of them and carried them over to the table. He set them down, then opened the first one.

"This is a translation of an account written by a monk from China many centuries ago," he explained. "The monk traveled to the city where the creature was rumored to live and spent several days observing the locals. He gathered information about the monster and the people surrounding it. He also collected reports of sightings from other travelers and monks.

"After his trip, the monk published this account. It tells the story of a man attacked in the woods near his home. He was traveling alone when he was suddenly approached by a huge beast. It was covered in black fur and stood taller than five men. Its eyes glowed yellow, and it had fangs larger than a child's arm. It screamed at him and then attacked.

"The man was severely injured, but he managed to escape. He returned to his village and told everyone what had happened. He told them that this was a monster and that it was coming for them. Everyone ran away, terrified.

"Soon, the villagers began to die. They were attacked in their homes while sleeping and while traveling along the road. None of them survived. As the attacks continued, the people grew desperate. They begged the monk to send help, but he refused.

"I cannot, he wrote. I have seen the foul creature myself. It is real, and it will continue to kill unless we destroy it."

"Eventually, the man convinced the monk to join forces with him. Together, they went to confront the beast, armed only with their swords. When they arrived, the monster was already in the middle of a battle with another warrior.

"Both men fought bravely, but neither managed to slay the other. Instead, they began to fight over who would win. With each passing second, the beast grew stronger and more powerful. Eventually, they became exhausted, and both fell unconscious.

"When they awoke, the monster was gone. It had wandered off into the night, leaving behind a pile of dead bodies. The monk decided to take the bodies with him, but when he reached the town, he discovered that everyone had fled. They had been afraid of the creature and had run away.

"He buried the bodies in a nearby field and returned to the monastery. For the rest of his life, he dedicated himself to fighting against the beast that had killed his friends and family. He spent the next decade searching for it and writing about it in his journals. His last entry told how he had found and defeated the creature. He described it as a giant wolf that ate everything in sight.

"He said that if anyone wanted to defeat it, they should go into the forest and stay there until it was dark. Then, wait for the moon to rise. If you can do this, then you will see it clearly. It's large and covered in thick black fur. Its eyes glow yellow, and it has sharp fangs."

He finished reading the passage, put the journal down, and looked at her. "That's all I have,' he said. "Do you want to look at some of them now?"

Chelsi nodded eagerly. "I want to know everything you can tell me about them!"

Alfredo smiled. He got up, and went into his bedroom. He came back a moment later with a stack of papers. He set them down on the table, and picked up the first one.

"These are translations of the stories written by the monk," he explained as he flipped through them. "'The Monk Who Killed the Beast,' 'Monk vs. Monster,' 'The Wolf of Death,' and 'The Moon-Touched Wolf.' These are all part of his journals."

Chelsi read through the titles. "Are these the only entries?" she asked.

"No," he answered. "There are hundreds of them. Most of them are short stories describing the monster encounters he'd had during his lifetime. There are also longer passages about the beast's history and the different cultures surrounding it. Here is a story from France. He handed her another paper. It was written in French and titled 'Le Chien de la Mort." She read through it quickly, then glanced up at him.

"In 1572, three monks traveled to the village of Saint Pierre in France. They were there to investigate rumors about a strange creature that lived in the woods.

"On their journey, they heard stories about the monster's terrifying reputation. They met with several people who claimed that they had seen the creature and that it had killed a number of people.

"One day, they came upon a group standing outside a church. One of them told them they were there to bury the woman's body who had been killed by the creature. The monks paid their respects, then took a closer look at the corpse.

"Her skin was pale white and covered in scars, they wrote. She had been brutally mutilated. Her arms and legs had been torn off, and her face was missing entirely. Each finger had been cut off, and her tongue and genitals had been removed.

"They realized that she must have been a witch. But why would a monster kill a woman just because she was a witch? Could it be possible that the creature was trying to rid itself of witches once and for all?"

He stopped reading and looked at her. "That's the end," he explained.

Chelsi reread it. "Why did he cut off her fingers and tongue?' she asked. "Didn't he realize that he was destroying evidence?"

Alfredo shrugged. "I don't know," he admitted. "Maybe he was just trying to hide it from the villagers. Or maybe he thought that the cuts would make it easier for her to speak with the saints in heaven after she died.

"Anyway, they tried to talk to the villagers more, but they didn't understand anything being said. Finally, one of the villagers noticed the monks and shouted that they had brought death to their land. The monks decided to leave, and they went to the nearest town.

"It was there that they encountered an old priest. He seemed confused by their questions and offered no explanation. So, they left the next morning and headed towards Saint Pierre."

He closed the book. "That's it," he explained.

Chelsi took a deep breath. "What does it mean?"

"I'm not sure," he confessed. "But we may have found our next step."

She nodded. "Where do we go from here?"

He stood up, and retrieved a few more books from the table. "Well," he began, setting them down on the table. "These are all accounts of the same creature."

She looked through the titles. "The Wolf from Hell," "Livestock Slaughtering," "'The Werewolf of Poland," "Werewolf: A History."

"There's something about this particular creature," he explained. "It kills people, steals their livestock, and it's always hungry. That's what the villagers in France saw as well. It would sneak into towns and villages in the night and attack people. In the morning, it would steal whatever food it could find. It would eat until it was full, then leave.

"Each time it appeared; it would attack a different place. No matter where it went, it never stayed long. Sometimes, it would disappear for months at a time. It would reappear and terrorize another town. The people would begin to grow suspicious, and they grew angry.

"Finally, one day, they had enough. They organized an expeditionary force and marched into the forest. When they arrived, they found the monster in the midst of a feast. The monks told the villagers to retreat, and then they joined the villagers in hunting down the creature.

"They chased it through the forest, killing it with swords, arrows, and rocks. Once it was dead, they cut it open and examined its body. They discovered that it had a human's head but a wolf's body. Its eyes were yellow, like those of a wolf, and they had fangs that could easily tear through anything.

"At this point, they decided to burn the body. They lit a fire and threw it onto the flames. As the body burned, they discovered it was filled with black smoke. It smelt of sulfur and brimstone, and it emitted a foul stench.

"The villagers were horrified by what they had done and fled the area. Later, rumors circulated that the abomination was a demon. It was sent to earth by God as punishment for sin. And so, they believed that burning it was the right thing to do."

He looked at her, "Is this the creature we're looking for?"

She nodded enthusiastically. "Yes!"

He smiled. "Then that's the first step. Let's get started."

"What do you think, Mr. Stanford? You have been quiet throughout this discussion," Delacruz asked.

Ronald shrugged. "I am thinking that if we are going to kill a monster, then we need weapons."

"Ahh, I think I can help with that." Delacruz said with a smile. "Follow me."

Delacruz had a huge shed in the back of his property. Inside was row, after row of rifles, shotguns, handguns, knives, bows, spears, crossbows, and anything else he might need to hunt with or defend himself with.

"All these are loaded and ready to use," Delacruz said as he opened a drawer in his desk. "This is your payment for helping us kill the monster."

Ronald took the gun. It was a .44 Magnum revolver.

"Thank you," said Ronald. "I promise I will keep it safe."

"Let me show you the rest of my collection," Delacruz said. "There are more guns, bows, and knives in here."

***

CHAPTER 13

DOWNTOWN MIAMI, EVENING

Donna Sanchez made no apologies for her illegal employment as a call girl. It was, she said, an interesting job that kept her in touch with the kind of people who could make life worth living. Her clients were businessmen and lawyers, mostly middle-aged men, but she also had some younger ones: women who liked to play the field or young men who wanted their first taste of womanhood without parental disapproval. She didn't want anything from them except what they paid for—sex, usually only oral sex. The money gave her freedom; she didn't need to go back home or live in poverty like so many others did. And, she added, if it weren't for her clientele, she wouldn't have been able to pay for college.

She'd gone to school for communications, planning to become a reporter. She dropped out after two years when she found out that most reporters couldn't afford the rent on their apartments unless they had another source of income. So instead, she became one of the women in her clientele's "stable." She wasn't ashamed of what she did, and was proud that she managed to keep her grades up even though she worked full time and went to school part-time. One of the few things she regretted was having a child so young. Be that as it may, having her daughter was the best thing that had happened in her.

The baby girl was named Rosemary, Rosie for short.. The name came from an old boyfriend who had proposed by saying, "I'll love you till roses grow over your grave," which was very romantic since she didn't like roses much. She had really liked Enrique. He had died in a car accident coming home late one night after work. He'd been drinking and speeding, which was illegal but not uncommon around there. All of the local bars were close, and people often drove home drunk. She had taken his death hard. It was such a waste. His parents blamed her because he was supposed to be at home with her when the accident happened. Even though it was his fault, they felt that she should have stopped him.

"Oh well," thought Donna, "such is life, as they say."

"You're a very pretty girl," he told her. "Your face is striking; your figure is well proportioned.

You don't look old enough to have graduated from college."

"I'm twenty-four."

"And you've spent your entire professional life working in this business?"

She laughed and shook her head. "No, I do other jobs. Just because I sell my body doesn't mean I can't use it for something besides pleasure."

"What else are you good at?"

She shrugged. "Asking questions, telling stories, writing nice letters that say, 'Thank you for allowing me to spend the weekend with you.'"

Dimitri nodded and smiled. "That sounds impressive." He took a seat across the table from her.

"My name is Dimitri Ivanovich," he said.

"Dima . . . ?" Donna asked hesitantly. "Is that Russian?"

He smiled again. "Yes, it's Russian."

She stared at him for a moment before speaking. "How long have you been in America?"

"Thirty years," he answered.

"Are all Russians like you? Rich?"

"Mostly. Some are poor, yes, but most are rich."

"But you're different from them," Donna went on.

"Why do you say that?" He asked.

"Well, you don't dress like them. You must be very wealthy."

He laughed. "I am, but I still wear jeans and sneakers."

"Oh. So why did you come here?" she asked. "Surely there are plenty of places where you can find beautiful women to satisfy your needs. Or, if not, you can always go back to Russia."

Dimitri thought about his answer before giving it. "This country has more opportunities than any other place in the world. I'll never grow bored living here."

"And you think that will last forever?" Donna inquired.

"Of course. Why wouldn't it?" He responded.

"Because nothing lasts forever." Donna said with confidence.

"You can't know that," Dimitri challenged her.

"I do. The future is uncertain and it's much better to plan for whatever happens rather than wait around until it does. My mother died of cancer when she was only forty-seven. My father taught me how to live my life. I learned what I needed to know in order to survive. Now I'm teaching my daughter. If she survives, she'll be able to deal with anything that comes her way."

"And you think your daughter is destined for the same fate?"

"Not necessarily. But she might encounter the same problems I did growing up. If she does, she'll learn to deal with them."

Dimitri looked down at his cup of coffee. "Is that why you're doing this?"

Donna sat back in her chair and raised her eyebrows. "Doing what?"

"Selling yourself. For money."

"Yeah, I guess it is. It's not like I'm getting married anytime soon, you know."

"But you wouldn't marry somebody just because he was rich."

She laughed. "Of course not! What a silly thing to suggest!"

"Then why would you make love to a man for money?"

"It's not the same thing, Dima. Men aren't possessions."

He nodded. "True, but women are."

"Of course, they are. That's why they sell themselves—to get married."

"That is not true."

Donna frowned and glanced over at the door. "Who's here?"

Dimitri lowered his voice. "The police."

"Oh shit. They must be looking for someone," Donna said with trepidation.

"They probably are," he responded.

"Well, let's hope they don't ask too many questions," she whispered. "I don't want to talk to anyone, especially the cops."

"Me either."

Donna quickly stood up and grabbed her purse off the counter behind the bar.

"We should go somewhere more . . . private, do you know such a place?" he asked.

Donna shook her head. "Sorry, no. But I'll take you wherever you want to go."

"Good enough. Let's get out of here," he said, licking his lips.

She followed him out of the restaurant.

"Where are we going?" she asked.

"Just follow me," Dimitri answered.

She looked around to see if anyone was watching them, but the streets were deserted. Soon they reached an alleyway between two apartment buildings. Dimitri stopped and turned around to face her. "Shall we?" he asked. Donna stepped forward and took his hand.

It was about a two in the morning in Downtown Miami last time Donna had checked the time. Normally, she didn't follow Johns into dark alleys, but she couldn't afford to be around for uncomfortable questions from the cops. Besides, this guy looked like he had some money. Maybe if she put it on him good enough, he would become a repeat customer. She led him through the shadows of the alley and down the side of the building to the end. There was a dumpster there, covered with graffiti.

"Are you down with screwing here?" He asked. "I don't know how much longer I can wait."

She smiled. "You do this often, don't you?"

"All the time."

"So you're used to waiting."

"Screw you."

She moved closer to him and placed her hands on his shoulders. "Let's get this over with. I'm tired."

He grabbed her by the arms and pulled her close to him. "No way, bitch. You don't decide when I finish."

"I can tell you right now that you're going to finish before I do," she said.

"I couldn't agree more," he said. His eyes changing color. "If you've got what it takes, then give it to me."

"OK, OK, enough already," she said. "Let's get this over with."

She unzipped her blouse and let it fall open. It was then she realized that she had made a horrible mistake!

Dimitri's paw lashed out and tore a piece of flesh out the left side of her face! His claws ripping through her skin left her feeling like she was being disemboweled! The pain was unbelievable, and she felt herself losing consciousness. All she wanted to do was die. She tried to pull away from him, but he was stronger than she was and she couldn't break loose. She closed her eyes, waiting for the end to come. It never did. Instead, he continued tearing at her body while she lay there, helpless.

Finally, he stopped and looked down at his handiwork.

"Now that's what I call service!" he said.

There were deep lacerations all over her chest and stomach, and a gaping hole where her left breast once was. Blood began pouring out of it as he ripped through her clothes, exposing her naked form to the night air. Then he bent down and started licking the blood from her wounds. After a few minutes, he stopped and stood up. She watched him walk past her, and turn back around to face her. He sniffed her body, tasting the blood on her skin before finally looking back at her.

"Have you ever seen anything so beautiful?" he asked.

Donna opened her mouth to respond, but no words came out. Her jaw had been broken during the attack, and she could barely breathe. She looked to her legs, which were also bleeding profusely. The tip of his claw had torn through the skin, and her flesh hung loosely from the bone. He walked over to her and leaned down so that their faces were inches apart. He could smell the scent of her fear.

"I want you to know that I really enjoyed myself," he said. "You were very good."

Donna gurgled a response, but that was all. She was slipping into unconsciousness. His face was changing. His features becoming more defined. His head grew bigger and the muscles in his neck bulged. He reached down with his left hand and grabbed her by the hair. His snout was elongating, dark fur started growing on this face, arms, and hands. His eyes had completed their change, gold and yellow in color. Slowly, he pulled her to her feet and brought her over to the wall next to the dumpster. He pushed her against it and began licking her face. She tried to push him away, but she was weak and couldn't move. He licked her lips, cheeks, nose, and ears before moving down to her neck.

He lapped up the blood that was running down from the wound on her throat. Finally, he lifted his head and looked at her. She saw the fangs protruding from his lower lip. The last thought Donna had before she was decapitated was that she hoped she raised her daughter to be smarter than she was.

***

CHAPTER 14

HOMESTEAD, MORNING

Ronald woke up the following day and got dressed. He walked out of the house and headed toward the shed. His heart was pounding, and he wondered if he was doing the right thing. He was going to kill a monster.

His hand gripped the gun tightly, and he looked at it for a moment. What have I gotten myself into? he asked himself. He had thought he would never be exposed to the supernatural again after what happened to him in the desert, but that was another story.

Delacruz took a deep breath, "How are you feeling?"

Ronald looked at him. "I feel fine," he answered. "Ready to do this."

Delacruz smiled. "I want to say thank you. You've given me a lot of hope, and I think you will help us greatly. I just wanted to let you know that before we get started today."

Ronald nodded. "I'll keep that in mind," he replied.

Delacruz walked over to a rack of weapons. He pulled out a spear, then handed it to Ronald.

"Here," he said. "You ready?"

Ronald took a deep breath. "As ready as I'll ever be." Then Ronald took a seat in front of the door to the shed. Delacruz knelt down and sat beside him.

"I'm going to ask you to take a deep breath," Delacruz said. "Exhale slowly. Now, relax. Let all of your tension flow out of you."

Ronald did as he was told. *I've done this a hundred times*, he thought. The last time he had gone through this exercise was behind a high-powered sniper rifle.

"Now, imagine yourself walking through a field of flowers," continued Delacruz. "See the colors and smell the scent. Imagine every part of your body relaxing. Take as much time as you need. Remember, a warrior must always be clear of thought before the kill!"

Delacruz stood up, nodded at Ronald, then walked away without another word. Ronald could hear his footsteps receding into the distance. He sighed deeply, then closed his eyes, focusing on the scent of flowers wafting through the air.

He opened his eyes. His arms were crossed over his chest, his hands resting lightly on top of them. He stared at nothing in particular for a moment, then gently pushed himself to his feet.

The door was wide open now; light from inside the shed shined onto the ground. Ronald looked around outside. There were no signs of anyone approaching. He cautiously stepped inside. He found Delacruz sitting on a wooden chair. His head rested against the wall, and his legs stretched before him.

Ronald approached him and kneeled down so that they were eye to eye.

"You're too tense," Delacruz said. "It will not help you if you don't let go of it. You have to empty everything else out of your mind and focus only on what is coming."

"I know," Ronald replied. "But I can't help it."

"Yes, you can. That's why we are here. When you walk through that door, the only thing you should have on your mind is what you are doing. No more thinking about work or family or whatever else might distract you. Just you and the job."

Ronald nodded. "But even if I do that . . ."

"What?" asked Delacruz.

"Even if I do that, what if something else distracts me? What if my nerves get the best of me?

"What if I panic? With the shit I've seen. Let's just say I'm on edge a lot these days. I'm just really good at hiding it."

Delacruz shook his head. "No. You can't allow that. If you allowed that, then you would lose control, and you wouldn't be able to stop. It would be like a storm. All of your thoughts would come flooding out, and you would become lost in the chaos. We must prevent that from happening."

"I understand," said Ronald.

Just then, Chelsi walked into the shed. Delacruz looked at her solemnly. "There is one thing we haven't discussed, I don't know you very well, and I didn't want to scare you."

Chelsi smiled nervously. "What is it?"

Delacruz looked at her gravely. "I have worked with your kind before; in fact, years ago, I worked with your grandmother on several cases, so I know a little about your world. I remember her telling me something; I'm surprised she didn't tell you."

Chelsi's nervousness only increased. She thought she knew what he was going to say. She had been trying not to think about it until now.

"When you reach out in the void to touch another soul, that connection is a TWO-WAY STREET. Whatever you are looking at CAN LOOK BACK AT YOU! So . . . what I am saying is that now that you have been alerted to what is out there, it has also been alerted of YOUR existence! Whatever we are about to do, we should do it fast because I fear that as we prepare to go after it, it may be preparing to go after YOU!"

Ronald was stunned, but he quickly recovered. He saw the look of concern on Chelsi's face. By the look on it, Abuela HAD told her that! It was news to him though.

"Don't worry," he said reassuringly. "We will handle this, don't worry."

"Alright, I'll trust you; just make sure you don't screw up," she said, smiling.

Ronald took a deep breath and exhaled. Then, taking a step toward the door, he reached out and grabbed hold of the handle. He turned it, pushed open the door, and stepped out into the morning air.

Ronald stood in front of the shed, staring at the open door.

***

Miami Dade Police Department
Downtown Miami, evening

"So, what are you thinking?" Jane asked. "I didn't have a chance to ask him about this stuff when he called me."

Detective Simon Nicholls smiled at her. "Well, I'm not sure if there is anything we can do, but it certainly sounds like some kind of cult. It would be interesting to talk to one of them before they're caught to find out their motivation."

"Those are my thoughts exactly," she said, taking a sip from her glass of water. "Not sure how much good it will do us, though. We've got all these people dying in strange circumstances, and no one seems to know where they came from."

"We still have no suspects besides Stanford," Simon said. "I'm still trying to get more information on him. The company he works for now, and the Agency are being VERY tight-lipped. Do you think he is a part of this cult? Or a part of something else?"

She nodded. "Yeah, I think so. If he is involved or has any connection, I don't see why he wouldn't tell us what it is. And if he doesn't know, that makes it much more suspicious."

"Yes, but without evidence, I doubt we'll ever get anywhere. Nothing is tying him to anyone here."

Jane looked up at him. "Which brings me back to the cult thing. What kind of cult could be behind all this?"

"Good question, Detective Goodman," Simon replied. "I suppose it may be possible that someone in South Florida is trying to set up a new cult, but I find it hard to believe that they have hundreds of followers that nobody knows about."

"Well, let's hope you're right," she said. "In the meantime, we need to find out who, how and where everyone is connected. That way, we can stop the killer and catch the cult before they do."

Simon smiled. "You sound like you have it all figured out already."

She shrugged. "Just hoping to keep my mind off things. I guess we should start by talking to each person's family to ensure they aren't hiding anything and then check to see if they have any connections. Maybe they all came from the same town, or heard about it from a friend or something."

"Yes, that would be a good place to start," the Detective said, looking at his watch. "It's late now; let's meet again tomorrow and try and get a plan together."

"Okay, sounds good. Let me know when you've got some results on your end as well," Jane said, standing up and putting her coat on. "I'm sorry for what happened earlier today. It was just a little scary."

He grinned. "Don't worry about it; it happens. Now go home and get some rest. You look tired."

The following day, Jane woke up feeling refreshed after a full night of sleep. She had a plan for the day: call each person's family and ask them questions about their friends and acquaintances. After that, she'd do an internet search to see if any similar cases were happening elsewhere. By the time she was done, she hoped to have a better idea of who else might be involved with the cult.

After a quick shower and getting dressed, she grabbed her phone and headed downstairs. On the drive to work, she called the first name on the list, asking to speak to Mr. Fox's wife. To her surprise, Mrs. Fox answered.

"Hello?"

Jane cleared her throat nervously. "Mrs. Fox? This is Detective Goodman from the Miami Police Department."

There was a pause. "Oh, yes, hello. How can I help you?"

"I'm calling because I want to talk to Mr. Fox's son, Zack."

"I don't think he's around anymore." The woman sounded disinterested.

Jane waited patiently.

"We haven't seen him in weeks."

"Can I leave a message for him?"

"Sure, but I'm not sure he'll even bother to return it."

"Alright. Thank you."

Jane hung up and sighed. She had four more names to call before lunch, so she decided to skip breakfast and head straight to work.

When she arrived, she gave her partner a quick update on how things were going.

"So you found no connection between these people?" Abraham asked.

"No, sir, I didn't."

"That's too bad. Well, I assume you still want to continue?"

Jane nodded. "I think it's worth a shot."

"Then I guess we should call the next one," the Detective said, pulling out his cell phone.

Jane leaned over his shoulder and saw the number on the screen: 954-491-1245. She quickly dialed it. "This is Detective Goodman from the Miami Police Department," she began. "I want to speak with Mr. Gassman about the murders."

"Mr. Gassman isn't available. Can I take a message?" said a man's voice on the other end.

"Yes, please. Could you tell Mr. Gassman that Detective Goodman from the Miami Police Department would like to speak with him about the murders?"

"Sure, I'll pass along the message."

Jane thanked him and hung up.

"What did you say?" the Detective asked, looking at her.

"We need to speak with him about the murders," Jane repeated.

"Didn't you just talk to him this morning?"

"No, the last time I talked to him was yesterday," Jane explained. "So he could have been contacted since then."

"Do you remember his number?"

"No, sorry," Jane replied. "But I do have his family's number."

"Let's give them a try," the Detective suggested. He reached for his phone and dialed the first number.

"Hello, this is Mrs. Gassman. Who is this please?"

"My name is Detective Goodman from the Miami Police Department," Simonreplied "Is Mr. Gassman available?"

"No, he's away on business. May I ask why you're calling?"

"I'm trying to interview him about the murders."

"Oh, I see," Mrs. Gassman replied. "If you'd like, I'll have him contact you when he gets back."

"Thank you. We'd really appreciate it."

"Don't mention it. Have a nice day."

"You too, ma'am."

They hung up and looked at each other.

"Well, that was useless," Simon said.

"Maybe we should try his dad instead," Jane suggested.

"Sounds good. Give me two minutes," Simon said, dialing the second number.

As they waited, Jane took a seat at her desk and tried to figure out how to get in touch with Mr. Gassman herself. She needed to find out which of his many offices he worked from or where he went on business. If only she knew more about him.

Simon returned a few moments later and sat down beside her. "You still want to try contacting him?"

"Yes, please," Jane said, smiling at him.

He smiled back and called the third number. When the receptionist picked up, he told her he was calling to speak with Mr. Gassman about the murders.

"I'm sorry, sir, Mr. Gassman left earlier today. Did you want to leave a message?"

"Actually, I don't really need to speak with him. But I did notice that you sounded familiar." Simon paused for several seconds while he thought. "Is there any way I could reach your supervisor? Or is it just the person who handles all the calls?"

The woman hesitated again for several long seconds before replying. "May I ask why you're calling?"

"It's personal," Simon replied. "But this needs to be taken care of. Can you tell me when Mr. Gassman will return so I know when to call back?"

"Well . . . .I'm not allowed to give that information over the phone. But I do have his office address and telephone number. Would you like those?"

"That would be great!" Simonthanked her and hung up.

Jane leaned forward in her chair and asked, "What did you say to her?"

"I used my best Doctor Evil voice."

She laughed.

Simon shook his head and smiled. Then he turned serious and said, "Listen, Jane, maybe we should wait until tomorrow morning before trying to contact him again. This isn't going to go away anytime soon . . ."

"Right," Jane agreed. "You've got a better chance of getting through to him first thing in the morning than after a hard day of work."

Simon nodded and stood up. He reached into his pocket and pulled out a piece of paper with the address and telephone number written on it.

"I'll write down what you said. You can use it to call back tomorrow. That way, you won't have to worry about remembering exactly what to say."

"Thanks, partner," Jane said. "I appreciate it."

They both left the room and started walking toward the exit. As they passed the reception counter, Jane noticed the dark-haired woman looking at her curiously.

She stopped in front of the counter and smiled at the receptionist. "Good afternoon. I hope I didn't keep you from anything important."

The woman smiled back. "No, actually. I wasn't doing anything."

"Then I'm glad I caught you. I wanted to make sure you had the information I gave you earlier."

The woman read the note quickly, then looked up. "Oh, yes. Thank you, Miss Barstow. I'm sorry; I had completely forgotten about it."

Jane smiled and headed for the door without waiting to see if the woman followed her. Outside, she noticed Simon looking at her with a smile.

"See you tomorrow," she said.

Jane stayed late at the police station, working on reports and making copies of some of the evidence they'd collected. She had hoped to finish by eight but didn't quite manage it. The sun had already gone down, and darkness surrounded the building.

Jane finally finished putting everything together and slid the papers into the filing cabinet with the rest of her case files. She sighed deeply and leaned back in her chair.

Just then, someone knocked on her office door. She turned around to look out the window and saw it was the Simon Nicholls.

"Come in," she said.

He stepped inside and closed the door behind him.

"Do you mind if we talk outside?" she asked.

"Not at all."

They walked out onto the steps of the police station and sat down.

"I thought you were going home?" Simon asked.

"I'm leaving in a minute, but I wanted to check one last thing before I do."

"Okay. What is it?"

"I've been thinking about what you said earlier," Jane began. "About the fact that we haven't seen anything strange at the other murders yet. It got me wondering whether it might be a good idea to start checking the other sites." She said.

"And that's why you're still here?" He asked.

"Pretty much. I think it's possible that the killer may strike again before we even find a connection between these victims." Jane replied.

Simon nodded. "Maybe you're right. Maybe we should take a closer look at Stanford's place and look at the other crime scenes."

Jane shook her head. "I don't know about that; besides we have already combed every section of his house."

"Don't worry about that. I'll handle everything," Simon responded.

"What do you mean?" She asked.

"I told you, I've been thinking about this all night. I've come up with a plan."

Jane frowned. "I can't wait to hear this one! I am NOT trying to get caught up in something sketchy!

Simon laughed.""Don't worry, I think you'll like this," Simon said.

She looked at him suspiciously. "What makes you think that?"

"Let me show you something." The Detective reached into his jacket pocket and pulled out a small silver key with a chain attached. He held it up in the light and said, "This is my mother's house key. She lives two blocks from here."

Simon handed the key to Jane.

"Can you imagine how easy it would be for someone to steal this key?"

Jane took the key and examined it closely. "It looks pretty ordinary to me."

"People who are determined enough can break into almost any place. And they aren't always careful with their keys. They often lose them or drop them somewhere. I could have lost mine last week," he explained.

Jane looked at him. "So you think you're going to sneak into your mom's house by taking her key?"

"Of course not," he replied. "I'm going to use my own key."

Jane stared at him for a moment. "How do you know she doesn't have two identical keys?"

"I don't."

"All right, then., I guess I'll have to go along with you." Jane looked down at the key and said, "But I'm keeping this."

"If you're worried about the possibility of someone stealing your key, I can give you another copy."

"No thanks. There's no guarantee that whoever stole my key won't come back for it later. It's safer to keep it close to me, even though I have to carry it with me wherever I go."

Simon nodded. "I understand."

He leaned forward and placed his elbows on his knees. "So, what do you think of my idea?"

"Why don't you tell me first?" Jane asked.

"Sure. All right. My plan is this: We're going to drive to Stansford's place. I'll park the car across the street from his house. You will go in first to make sure the coast is clear."

"Wait, why do I have to be the one to go in first?" Asked Jane. "Why can't it be you?"

Simon laughed a little. "Okay. You have a point there, let's go in together. You're a real ball buster, you know that?"

Jane rolled her eyes in annoyance. "I'm not sure if I should take offense to your comment or not, but hey, boys will be boys, right?"

Simon responded with a laugh. "Well then, let's get this show on the road.

Are you ready to go now?"

"I think I am." Jane replied. "Let's do this and hope we don't get suspended.".

***

Miramar, Evening

Simon parked his car in the parking lot behind the old house on Highland Street. The street was quiet, and most of the homes on either side were dark. He turned off the engine and sat alone in the dark vehicle, watching the house across the street.

Jane came down the steps of the police station and walked toward his car. He opened the door for her and helped her get inside.

When they were driving toward the address on the GPS earlier in the evening, Simon felt a weight in his stomach. He knew it would be difficult to do this alone, but he also believed that Jane was the right person for the job. She had a natural instinct for this type of work, and he trusted her completely.

When they arrived at the address, he parked the car on the street. Simon looked at Jane briefly before turning off the car.

"Ready?" he asked. "You still have time to change your mind. I wouldn't want to be the one halting your rise to Chief of Police."

Jane hesitated for a moment before saying, "I'm ready."

"Okay," Simon said as he got out of the car and locked it. "Let's go see what we can find. Who knows, we may get a medal for this!"

Jane smiled and nodded. "I would settle for keeping my job, I can't count how many laws we are breaking right now."

Simon laughed. "No pain, no gain!" Simon said with a smile.

She nodded.

Simon reached into his pocket and pulled out a flashlight. He held it up in the air and turned it on.

"Be careful," Jane whispered.

"Yes. Just stay close to me." He said.

They climbed out of the car and stood beside it. The Detective shone his flashlight once more around the area.

"Ready?" he asked.

Jane nodded.

They crossed the street together and walked up the driveway. Simon shone his flashlight around the yard while Jane walked ahead of him. He followed her, shining his light ahead of them.

After entering the backyard, they walked through the grass. Simon stopped and pointed his flashlight ahead of him.

"Look at this," he said.

Jane looked where he was pointing and gasped.

There were several large puddles of blood on the ground.

"I don't understand. Why would you leave a trail of blood just lying here?"

"I don't know. But if it means something, the blood isn't fresh."

Jane looked at Simon, who shrugged his shoulders.

"Okay," Jane said. "What do we do now?"

"We're going to walk around the house." He drew his weapon. "You watch my back."

"And you watch mine." She replied.

They continued walking until they reached the front door. Simon looked apprehensively at Jane. "Go ahead and knock, I don't want to be here all night!" he chuckled.

Jane pushed open the door, it wasn't locked and stepped inside. The hallway was dark, and the only light came from the glow of the lamp on the table. Jane looked around the house, shining her flashlight everywhere she went, her weapon following her line of sight. Simon followed closely parallel to her.

She paused in front of an old dresser that was covered with junk mail and magazines. She looked at the floor beneath it.

"Oh, my God!" she exclaimed.

"What is it?" Simon asked.

Jane examined the floor in front of the dresser carefully. "Something happened here," she said. "Someone tried to hide evidence."

Simon watched her closely. "What do you mean?"

"I don't know. But I found some footprints leading away from here."

Simon looked at the prints on the floor. They led toward the kitchen.

Jane grabbed her cell phone from her pocket. "I'm calling it in; we will explain it to the Captain later." Jane hung up the phone after calling it in and put it back in her pocket.

"What's wrong?" Simon asked.

"I see a set of footprints leading to the back door. I think they were made by someone who was running away from the scene of the crime."

"Are you sure?"

"Yes. Look at them." She showed him the footprints on the floor. "See how they lead into the kitchen?"

"Those footprints definitely belong to someone who left the scene," Simon said. "But what about the other footprints?"

Jane glanced at him and said, "These are different. They were made by someone who entered the house."

She pointed to another pair of footprints near the kitchen. "There's a person standing right here and looking at the dead body."

Simon walked over to the footprints and saw that they were still wet. "Do you think these belong to the killer?"

"I don't know. But it sure looks like it."

The pair collectively stopped breathing when the heard the door bell ring.

"Don't move a muscle!" Simon hissed.

"What?"

"I don't think they can see us from here, but if we make any noise and attract attention then it could get very messy."

Ignoring Simon's order, Jane walked toward the door, pistol at the ready. Glowering at her, Simon walked to the window and peeked outside. He saw two men dressed in black suits and sunglasses standing in the driveway. One of them was holding a clipboard. The other one carried a camera and took pictures of the house.

"What do you think?" The Detective asked.

Jane shook her head and said, "I have no idea."

"Can we talk to them?"

"Probably not," she replied. "Our department doesn't allow civilians to question suspects or witnesses without authorization."

"Are you sure they are civilians?" Jane looked at Simon questioningly

The Detective sighed. He turned back to the window and watched the men as they moved around the property, taking pictures.

"I wish we knew what they were doing here," the Detective said. "I have a bad feeling about this."

Jane nodded. "Me too."

"What are we going to do?" Simon asked.

"I don't know," Jane said. "Let's wait and see what happens."

"If we can't talk to them, will we be able to find out who they are?"

Jane smiled sadly and said, "I don't know."

Simon looked at her. "You're not helping."

Jane frowned and said, "Sorry. But I'm trying to be honest."

He sighed and said, "Yeah, I know."

The Detective looked at the men in the driveway again. "They're leaving."

Both turned their attention to the front door. The first man on the sidewalk in front of the house, carried a large duffel bag and paused in front of the building, looking around. He paused in the front of the building and looked around. He placed the duffelbag on the ground and began opening its contents. He pulled out a small notebook and flipped through the pages. He stopped at the last page and looked at it briefly before putting the book away. Then he picked up the duffelbag again and walked back to the sidewalk. The second man walked past the house and headed toward the street.

"Who the hell are those guys?" Simon asked.

"I don't know. But I'm sure we'll find out soon enough. They look like Feds to me. Stansfield's file said he had worked for The Agency before he got into the scumbag babysitting business."

Jane had heard about The Agency, but she thought that the stories about the outfit were mostly rumors.

The Agency, not to be confused with the Central Intelligence Agency, the CIA, or any other spy organization, was a government organization whose charter allowed them to work in and out of the United States, unlike the Federal Bureau of Investigation, FBI, or the CIA. The Agency's task force consisted primarily of former military personnel and were highly trained in all manner of warfare, from hand-to-hand combat to weapons, explosives, vehicles and more, as well as being experts in many areas of human intelligence gathering, including interrogations, infiltration, surveillance and even assassination. They also had a large fleet of aircraft at their disposal, allowing them to quickly and covertly travel around the world, on missions both domestic and foreign.

An agent was never officially assigned to an area, unless it happened to fall under his jurisdiction. But if an agent received a request for assistance from another country or agency, or local enforcement, they would make contact with that agency or nation's representative to find out what they needed help with and where. If it wasn't something the agent could do themselves, then they'd either enlist the aid of one of their colleagues who was better suited for the job, or they'd simply refuse the mission. Some operatives may have been essentially mercenaries by nature, but there were limits even they wouldn't cross. That said, sometimes things just happened and you ended up in a bad place without knowing why. And when that happens, you just had to take your chances.

Simon studied the men as they walked away. "Don't worry. We'll figure this out."

"Oh Yeah," she agreed. "We definitely will."

They sat side by side on a bench outside the police station. After talking to Jane, the Detective drove her back to her apartment. When he dropped her off, he thanked her for helping him.

"Well, that was an interesting date," she replied with a smile.

"I know you had doubts, but I'm glad you came along. I wouldn't have been able to do this without you," Simon said.

Jane gazed down at her feet and said nothing.

"I just wanted you to know that I appreciate you riding shotgun," Siman said awkwardly. "Don't let it go to your head or nothing, I'm not proposing marriage."

She laughed softly, then looked at Simon with an arched brow and said, "Really? Thanks, I'll try to take your praise graciously. To be honest, it was kinda fun."

Simon smiled and patted her hand. "So, what are you going to do now?"

"Go home," she replied. "Take a hot shower and get some sleep."

"Sounds good."

"Then maybe I'll go out tomorrow night. Not to a bar or anything. Maybe I'll meet some friends at a coffee shop somewhere. You know."

Simon nodded. "I hope you enjoy yourself."

Jane smiled and said, "Thank you. I will."

They sat in awkward silence for a moment and looked at each other. Then the Detective turned away from her and pulled out his cell phone, as it rang.

"Simon," he answered, then listened intently to whoever was on the other side of the call. When the caller finished, Simon replied, "Got it." He ended the call and looked at Jane. "I have to go. There's something I need to take care of."

"Okay," Jane said. "I'm heading back inside, see you later."

***

Chapter 15

Homestead, Chelsi's apartment, evening

Chelsi pulled into the parking lot of her apartment complex. As usual, she saw the same cars parked in the reserved spots. She wondered why anyone would bother to take a spot reserved for someone else. She laughed to herself thinking about the arguments that went on between neighbors over the right to park in a designated space. To her, it was almost funny.

As she walked towards the front entrance, she noticed that her building looked different somehow. She had never paid much attention to the way it looked, but today, it seemed to look weird. She passed a couple of other residents going in and out of the front doors. They both greeted her with a nod, but they didn't smile or anything. Her steps slowed as she approached the door, and she suddenly became aware of the noise of the outside world that been absent from her surroundings since she woke up. She turned and looked around. Everything appeared normal. A squirrel was watching her intently from a tree across the courtyard.

Chelsi entered the lobby then walked down the hallway towards the end of the hall. It was then that her body began to shiver as a chill ran up her spine. She stopped in her tracks, and suddenly became afraid. She scanned the hall, trying to find the source of the feeling in her body. She felt something in the air, something invisible, yet palpable. She felt it. She heard a low growl from somewhere, and there was a sensation of heat in the air.

"Who is that?" She whispered urgently. "Where are you? I can feel you . . . You're here."

She took deep breaths and tried to calm herself, but the feeling continued to increase. Her heart beat faster, and her hands started to shake. It wasn't just fear now; it was rage. She turned quickly towards the exit.

Her legs were strong, she only slowed once as she passed through the doors into the parking lot. Then she slowed and stopped, breathing heavily. She looked around at the few other cars parked by the building and then lifted her head, scanning the area beyond. Nothing. Just a small group of people walking past the restaurant. She breathed a sigh of relief, wiped the sweat off her forehead with the back of her hand, and moved to the front of the building, where she sat on the hood of her car and leaned forward, her hands resting on the metal.

For a minute, she thought about abandoning her plan to lure the Beast in. But then she remembered what had happened when she'd let herself get distracted in the past. The momentary euphoria of doing nothing had always turned into regret. And that's why she needed to stay focused on the task at hand—to find the monster so it couldn't kill anyone else. If she did that, maybe things would eventually return to normal.

"No, I have to do this. It's the only chance we'll get".

She didn't know how long she sat there, but finally, she stood up and shook her hair. She felt exhausted but exhilarated too. She thought about going back home but instead decided to see if she could find any traces of whatever it was that had been following her. She left her car and began to walk, pushing down the dread that came over her when she was alone.

As she made her way through the streets, she paused occasionally, staring intently at the shadows of trees or the corners of buildings. She saw nothing, heard nothing, smelled nothing. She kept looking, though, and she found herself near the center of town, closer to the center of campus. There were more people there, which made her feel safer. She turned a corner and immediately became aware of a presence behind her. She spun around quickly but again saw nothing.

"You're still here," she said. "Do you have a name? Can you talk to me?"

There was no response, but she knew he was there. She felt him.

She turned and started walking briskly, not slowing down until she reached the library. As she got close, she noticed a man sitting in one of the chairs outside. He was reading a newspaper, his eyes flitting from page to page. She approached slowly, stopping short of the chair so she wouldn't disturb him.

"Hello," she said softly.

He did not look up from his paper, nor did he respond. She stood watching him for a moment before giving up and turning away. She walked back toward the center of campus and stopped in the middle of the sidewalk. Looking around, she realized that the feeling she had felt earlier was gone. She wondered what it meant. Was it just the wind?

She looked at her watch and then turned and began to retrace her path. She had only gone a short way when she heard voices approaching from behind her. She turned and saw two young men walking towards her, their eyes fixed on her chest as they passed. She watched them go, anger welling up inside her. She could feel it, like heat radiating from an oven. She had to get out of there. She had to go somewhere else.

She hurried along the sidewalk, passing the bookstore and a convenience store. Taking the next turn, she walked toward the school's administration building. As she neared her destination, she could hear laughter coming from inside the building. She slowed and then stopped, unsure whether she wanted to continue. The sounds grew louder, and she could tell they were students. She turned and began to walk away when she suddenly remembered the last time she had come this way.

She turned back and began making her way to the entrance of the administration building, where the voice had first called out to her. She had walked into the main office but had found no sign of anyone. She began to leave when someone spoke. "Hey!" the voice had shouted.

"Hey, Cheelllsi! A male voice called, with an accent she couldn't place. Eastern European, Russian maybe.

It had startled her, and she jumped slightly. She hadn't recognized the voice but had thought it might be one of the students who worked in the office. She turned around to answer, but the person had vanished. Chelsi made her way to the building that housed the classrooms.

The doors were open. Inside there was a deep silence. The students seemed all gone. She walked up the stairs to the second floor and stood at the edge of the hall looking out into the empty room. There was no one about. She ran down along the hallway to the main entrance where she found the door wide open. She stepped inside and looked around. No one was here either.

She crept further inside, looking for signs of life. The silence was unnerving. It was as if everyone had just disappeared, or maybe she had simply missed them. Perhaps they had been called away by the sound of the bell. She closed the door behind her again, this time more quietly than before, then continued forward with her head down, watching her feet as she moved. A few paces further and she stopped at the wall by the stairwell. There was a door on the other side of the wall. She pressed her ear against it, listening intently.

There was nothing but silence from within.

If she went in here, she would be certain to find him. She drew breath and stepped inside, closing the door behind her.

The room was empty except for a single desk. She walked over to it and sat down, looking around. The room was mostly dark, the only light coming from the window above the door. She looked out the window but couldn't see much. She turned to face the door and then froze. She heard the laughter again, and she could feel it. It was right there. She could sense it, almost taste it. She leaned forward and put her hand against the wall, trying to push aside the feeling of dread. She didn't want to do this, but she knew she had to. She needed to know.

She stood up and paced around the room, trying to think what to say. Finally, she sat down again.at the solitary desk. She knew she had to say something but didn't know what. She closed her eyes and took a deep breath.

"I'm sorry," she said, opening her eyes. "This isn't right. But I need to know why you're here. Why are you doing this? Why are you following me?"

Still, there was no response, but she felt the presence behind her. It was still there. She waited, but nothing happened. She was afraid to turn around and look because she didn't want him to disappear.

"Please," she pleaded. "For God's sake, just tell me what you want!"

Again, there was nothing. She tried to remain calm but could feel the anger growing inside her. She couldn't stand it anymore. She had to see it. She turned and looked at the door.

"You know why you were looking for me, soooo . . . HERE I AM!"

With that, she bolted off the desk and ran to the opposite side of the room, leaning against the wall and trying to catch her breath. She couldn't believe she had done that. How stupid could she be? She had practically screamed at the presence, why was she surprised at the response?. She felt foolish. Despite everything that had happened, she still wasn't sure who or what was pursuing her. Was it the being from her vision? Or something else. She had to know!

She was still trying to calm herself when she heard the door open. She turned and saw the woman she had seen in the office walk into the room. She was smiling, but it looked forced.

"What's wrong?" she asked. "Why are you crying? Are you hurt?"

"No," Chelsi said. "I'm fine."

"Well, why are you crying? Are you lost young lady?"

Chelsi shook her head, unable to speak. The woman put her hand on Chelsi's shoulder and squeezed gently.

"Are you sure everything's alright?

Chelsi nodded.

"Well, I'm still not totally sure what's going on here young lady, but I'm sure I can help. Let me call someone and see if they can come by and take a look at you."

Chelsi shook her head again.

"No," she said. "It's not that. I am fine. And to be honest, you wouldn't believe me if I told you."

The woman frowned and chewed on her lip.

"It's okay," Chelsi said. "Really. It doesn't matter. Thanks for your help ma'am."

She stood up and moved to the door, pulling the handle and looking through the glass pane to ensure it was locked. Chelsi then took out her phone and called the number to the burner phone she had purchased for Ronald earlier. He was at Delacruz's place, out of the attention of law enforcement. He answered on the first ring. "Where are you? Are you ok? I lost you after you left the center of town!"

"I guess my batshit crazy idea worked." said Chelsi. She laughed nervously as she cleaned the tears off her face. Whoever, or whatever is after me came out in the open. Come pick me up, then we can move to the next step of the plan.

2 hours earlier

Chelsi's hands were shaking. What she had done tonight was very reckless; she knew that. When she had initially pitched the plan to Ronald and Delecruz earlier in the day, they vehemently disapproved the course of action. But they both grudgingly acquiesced to her plan when she pushed the point that there weren't many other options available but to lure the creature in to their turf so it could be killed in a location where they had the advantage

"Are you sure about this? Are you certain it will work?" asked Delecruz had asked.

"Yes." Chelsi paused for a minute before continuing. "It has to work. We have no time left to waste. The more we delay, the more people are going to get hurt. This is our only shot at getting rid of it once and for all," said Chelsi.

Delacruz nodded his head slowly. He stared off into space as if he was having trouble focusing. Ronald sat across from Chelsi; he was silent, watching. "We'll just have to hope everything goes according to plan. If not . . ." Delecruz trailed off as he contemplated the worst-case scenario.

"You don't need to worry about me," said Chelsi. "I can take care of myself just fine."

Delacruz didn't respond. Chelsi was grateful for his silence. She knew that Delecruz was worried about her, but she also knew that she had to see this through. Neither of them talked about what would happen if things went badly.

Chelsi sighed. "This is the only way."

"What if it doesn't work?"

Chelsi shook her head. "We have no other choice. I'm doing this for everyone's sake. This thing will just just keep killing if WE don't stop it."

"But what if something happens to you? I won't be able to protect you."

Chelsi smiled. "Don't worry, I'll be okay." She glanced at him. "I promise. Just be close when I call you."

Shadows covered Delacruz's cabin. It was dark outside, and Delacruz switched on the lights.

"Do you know how to use a gun?" asked Delacruz.

"No, but I've watched enough movies to know how to aim one."

"Good. That's all I need."

Chelsi sat down at the dining table. She pulled out a box of shells and began loading the weapon. Delacruz stood in front of the window, staring out into the darkness. "Where are the silver bullets?" Chelsi laughed. "Or is that just Hollywood bullshit?" After a few seconds, he turned around and walked toward Chelsi. She stopped what she was doing and looked up at him.

"Only fire or dismemberment can kill these monstrosities. Speaking of killing, are you ready?" he asked.

"I've come too far to go back now." replied Chelsi.

Ronald and Chelsi walked toward her car, where Ronald held the door open for Chelsi.

That was two hours ago.

Chelsi hoped they would have another chance to take a crack at that evil bastard before they all got killed.

The lovely lady that comforted Chelsi earlier had volunteered to escort her to Ronald 's car with a security guard. The lady and the guard had no idea the level of risk they had taken to help her meet up with Ronald; she was very grateful to them. When Ronald drove to pick her up, she could feel the disapproval and apprehension oozing off him. She knew he had disapproved of her plan from the beginning. Chelsi said nothing; that would be a conversation for another time, if there was another time! They both remained silent and alert during the drive back to her car, and now they were both in their perspective vehicles heading back to Delacruz's home.

Ronald looked in his rearview mirror; he had seen the tail ten minutes ago. He gathered his thoughts about what needed to be done next. Ronald knew that whatever or whoever had tried to attack Chelsi was probably close and on their tail. Though Chelsi had managed to escape its clutches, he didn't know how she had been able to do so, or if she thought her reckless plan would actually work. Ronald 's immediate concern had been finding her and bringing her home safely.

When they finally got to the house, Ronald got out of the truck and walked around to open the door for Chelsi. She leaned forward to reach her hand for him but then quickly straightened back up when she saw his expression. "What is it?" she asked.

"Keep your head on a swivel. You're not safe yet," he told her.

She looked at him quizzically, confused by his words. "Head on a swivel? What the hell does that even mean?"

When Ronald pulled the car up to the house and they both exited the vehicle, he was all business.

"I want you to get into the house as quickly as possible," Ronald said with conviction."When you get in there, tell Delacruz what I told you, and then don't move or do anything until I tell you!"

He reached into his pocket and pulled out some kind of pistol. Chelsi stared at it, uncomprehending as he held the weapon up for her to see. The weapon was blocky and made out of some kind of material that Chelsi suspected wasn't metal. The weapon didn't seem to have a safety either."This is a Glock 22, a very dependable sidearm, Delacruz lent it to me. I hope we live long enough for me to return it to him."

Chelsi took a step back from him; she couldn't believe what was happening. A gun in her face. She had never even touched one before. In fact, the thought of touching one was terrifying. The look on his face said that he was prepared to use it.

Her eyes went wide with terror.

"Don't worry, it's just for protection. Do you understand? Just don't move and help Delacruz get the weapons ready, you hear me?"

She nodded slowly.

"Okay, let's go inside," Ronald said as he led her to the porch and through the front door. Once inside, he again put his hand on her shoulder, and together they walked down the hallway toward the dining room. "Delecruz, I think that thing followed us up here!"

He was standing behind a counter next to the kitchen sink, looking out the window in front of him.

Ronald stood over him, blocking his view from outside, and looked out of the window himself. There was nothing visible; everything seemed normal, but he couldn't shake the feeling that something was watching them.

"Where are you going?" Delecruz asked.

"To see if we have any more trouble," he replied.

They both stepped around Chelsi and left the kitchen. As soon as they passed the doorway, he grabbed his gun off the small table near the entrance and slipped it into his pocket. They moved through the living room, which had no furniture other than one chair in the corner, and entered the front bedroom. The only thing in the room was a dresser and a bed with two mattresses. There was also an open closet door along the wall, so he opened it up and looked inside. Nothing was hidden in there, either.

Ronald turned around to make sure Delacruz was still following before he closed the closet door. He then walked back over to him. "Nothing here either," he said.

The two men made their way out of the room and headed down the hallway to the second bedroom. Again, no obvious sign of anything unusual was present. The house was empty—nobody except for the three of them.

When they got to the end of the hall, Ronald stopped, pocketed his Glock in the waistband of his jeans, and picked up a shotgun propped against the wall.

He opened the last door at the far end and stepped into the master bedroom. When he did, he noticed that it was completely dark. He flipped on the light switch, but nothing happened. He looked around the room and saw that the windows were covered with heavy curtains. He could barely see the outline of the bed he had been sleeping in less than twenty-four hours ago.

Ronald walked toward the bed and sat down on it. He turned around and looked at Delecruz, standing in the doorway, staring at him.

"What?" Ronald whispered.

The other man looked away and shook his head. "I'm sorry—"

"For what?"

"It's just . . .you look like you're expecting someone to jump out at us or something."

"Well, yeah," Ronald answered. "You should've seen the look on your face when I told you to hide behind me. You thought I was crazy. Well, maybe I am a little."

Delacruz smiled at him as he came over and sat down next to him. "I think I would prefer that, than to be attacked by a monster that can turn invisible or something."

Ronald laughed but was serious about not wanting to see anyone else killed. If that thing was stalking them, he wanted to be prepared.

He looked up at the ceiling and said, "So what do we do now?"

"We wait until morning and see if it comes after us again. If it does, we'll try to stay ahead of it. After that, we follow its trail, wherever that may lead us."

They didn't get a chance.

Just as Ronald finished speaking, a loud crash came from somewhere in the house. Both men jumped up from where they were sitting and ran toward the source of the noise. When they got to the living room, they found the front door shattered and lying on the floor. The jagged edges of the broken wood had been driven deep into the carpet, but most of the splinters had already been pulled out.

Ronald checked the breech of shotgun, to make sure is was loaded, then checked his Glock semi automatic pistol in his waistband and backup revolver pistol at his ankle were secured, and stepped through the doorway as Delacruz hurried into the room behind him. They both looked in every direction, trying to determine if anything was moving nearby. There was nothing to see, but they could hear the sounds of footsteps walking around inside the house.

"Wait here," Ronald whispered, and he rushed over to the front door and pushed what was left of the wrecked door, taking care to stay well out of sight against the wall next to the door, presenting a small target, or silhouette for whatever the hell was out there waiting to come in. He was not going to make it easy for It.

A gust of wind blew in, carrying with it the smell of fresh rain, but it wasn't enough to keep the air in the house from getting stuffy. The cold night breeze felt good against his skin, and he breathed deeply to calm his nerves. After a moment of listening, he stepped out from behind the wall to get a better look outside.

That was when he was brought face to face with the Beast.

It was standing directly in front of him, just inside the doorway. Its fur glistened in the moonlight that shone down upon it, reflecting off the wet wood decking beneath its feet. Its eyes were yellow and gold, and they burned brightly as it stared at him with hatred.

Ronald didn't hesitate; he pointed the shotgun and fired. The beast stumbled backward, falling to the ground with a cry. The bullet had hit it right in the chest, and it writhed in pain. But it quickly recovered and stood up again.

Ronald fired once more, this time hitting the Beast in the shoulder. It cried out again, but not in pain. Its howl echoed throughout the open field.

It charged forward, growling menacingly.

Ronald reloaded the shotgun, aimed at its head, and squeezed the trigger. This time, Ronald lost his footing and the recoil threw the weapon over his shoulder and nearly sent him sprawling to the ground. The shot missed, and the wolf dove toward him.

He searched frantically, but the shotgun was gone.

Ronald was going to reach for his Glock pistol, but the wolf lunged at him, and Ronald tried to dodge back, but it was much faster than he expected. The animal caught him by surprise and knocked him down onto the wet wood. He rolled over and tried to push himself up, but the wolf was on top of him before he could stand. He was pinned underneath its weight, unable to move or even breathe. Then the wolf was again rocked back by another shotgun blast!

Delacruz attempted to fire another round of hot buckshot into the Beast withRonald's fallen shotgun but was savagely hit with a paw that sent him crashing into the dining room.

"Damn!" Ronald shouted in anger and frustration as he got back to his feet and pulled out his backup revolver pistol out of its ankle holster. He drew back the hammer and aimed carefully, keeping one eye on the Beast and taking aim between its eyes. "Why won't you just die!" he screamed, pulling the trigger until he emptied all 6 rounds of the pistol into the Beast.

Shots rang through the night air and struck the beast square in the forehead. It collapsed once more . . . but got back up with blinding speed! It then turned toward Ronald with a snarl of rage!

"Son of a bitch!" Ronald yelled, dropping the revolver and looking around for something else to use against it. His gaze fell upon the spear Delacruz gave him earlier.

He grabbed it by the shaft, then began to run toward the Beast, screaming at the top of his lungs. It immediately sprang at him, but Ronald raised the spear high and brought it down hard into its chest. Ronald felt the impact of the stab reverberate through his arms, but he knew if he let go now, he was as good as dead.

He jabbed the spear into the Beast over and over, striking the Beast repeatedly until blood came gushing from its wounds. As he did so, he kept raising his strikes toward the beast's head. He wanted to get close enough to drive his blade into its brain, preferably. The Beast, still not down for the count,attacked him again, Ronald reversed the spear to the opposite end and caught it dead in the face.

Ronald kept jabbing the Beast the spear, which seemed to be working well. After another few blows, he saw that the beast was slowing down, bleeding profusely from its multiple stab wounds. Ronald attempted to go in for a kill shot to the Beast's head, but it moved at the last second, dodging the blow. Then, just as he thought he was about to finish it off, the Beast kicked out with its right foot.

Ronald's spear went flying out of his hands, and he stumbled back. Ronald's heart pounded in his chest as he struggled to escape, but the Beast was relentless. It tried to bite down on his leg; but Ronald continued to narrowly dodge its attacks.

Ronald had to think fast. He'd never felt so helpless before, and he was terrified that the Beast would kill him before he could find another weapon to subdue it. The Beast stood at its full height before him, dripping blood from multiple stab and bullet wounds to it's face and chest. It snarled at him menacingly and ran for him again. This time Ronald didn't have any choice but to dodge and run. The wolf chased after him with frightening speed. He could hear it coming, and as soon as he turned around, it was in prime position to pounce on him, ending the fight once and for all! Suddenly, a white light shot through the roof, the air around Ronald threating to knock him off his feet, and the Beast burst into flames!

There was a loud crack, and the animal screamed in agony as fire erupted from its body! The heat was intense, and it singed Ronald's hair and eyebrows as he struggled to pull away. He fell to the side, and the flames scorched the grass below him.

When the blaze was extinguished, Ronald looked up and saw that the beast had collapsed in a heap on the living room floor, writhing in pain. He watched as the animal began to convulse and twitch uncontrollably.

The transformation was almost complete. In seconds, the creature became a human being. He was tall and lean, with long dark hair and piercing green eyes.

"Ronald!" Delacruz shouted. "Get away from him!"

Ronald struggled to sit up and regain his bearings. His mind was spinning, and he had difficulty processing what had just happened.

But first, he had to help Delacruz.

He grabbed the man by the shoulders and helped him get back on his feet. He turned around and looked at the house as he followed Delacruz with his gaze. The front door was wide open, and smoke poured from the entryway. A few of the windows had been shattered by the gunfire, too.

The man was still on the ground. It wasn't moving anymore.

As Ronald glanced back at him, he saw Delacruz staring at the man on the ground.

"Are you okay?" he asked.

Delacruz's face remained blank. Then he looked back at Chelsi. Her eyes were glowing a silver hue. Behind her, he could see the outline of . . . something that looked like some kind of ancient warrior spirit. Then, it was gone. Chelsi's eyes returned to their earlier color.

"Chelsi?" Delacruz croaked, sounding confused. "What happened? What is going on here?"

She didn't respond. Instead, she turned around and walked over to the doorway that led into the house. She paused for a moment and looked back at Ronald and Delacruz before disappearing into the darkness.

"Chelsi?" Delacruz called again. But there was no answer.

Ronald knelt beside the body and examined it carefully. It was still alive, albeit in great pain, and it didn't look like it was in good shape. Its entire body was covered with third-degree burns. A large gash marred the left side of its face, while the front of its chest was covered in cuts and buckshot wounds. He looked at Delacruz, who had the shotgun in his hand. Ronald nodded, then moved back; Delacruz shot the creature multiple times with the shotgun. By the time he was done, there was nothing left resembling a human figure on the floor of his porch.

CHAPTER 16

HOMESTEAD, DELACRUZ'S HOUSE

The night was clear, the rain had stopped, but the wind had picked up. It blew in from the north, colder and sharper than it should have been for this time of year.

"Thank for saving my friends' and my life," Chelsi said to the Spirit.

"I did nothing," said the Spirit. "The power was always in YOU! It is your birthright. But there are those who would steal it from you. Do not let them. You have a gift to give, not just the gift of survival but also of change. Use this power wisely and well. Seek out others like yourself and help them find their own gifts."

"Will I see you again?" Chelsi asked.

"Who knows," the Spirit said. "Even I do not know the future," the Spirit said. A half smile played across its features. With that, the Spirit faded away.

Chelsi sat down by the dead tree killed by lightning and thought about what had happened. She was still shaking from her brace with death, but now that her adrenaline had worn off, she began to shiver and shake uncontrollably.

"You, okay?" I thought I heard you talking to someone," Ronald asked as he walked over next to Chelsi. He looked concerned.

"Yeah," Chelsi said in a voice so low it sounded almost like a whisper. "No, I'm not okay. I think I got hit by lightning."

Ronald laughed. "That's impossible; people don't get struck by lightning twice."

"Well, it just happened. I was standing right there, in the house, and then everything went black for a second, and I could feel all the hair on my body stand up straight, and then I felt hot and tingly."

"Oh wow, that's pretty crazy, but I wouldn't be surprised by anything after what happened tonight," Ronald said. Chelsi could hear the smile in his voice.

"What? What is wrong with you. Are you still shook?" Chelsi asked, looking at him suspiciously.

"Nothing, I'm joking. Don't be mad," Ronald said. "Though if you really did get struck by lightning, I wouldn't blame you for being a little upset."

"Don't be silly. That would mean I'd already died once, and I didn't. So, unless it's the same kind of bolt of lightning that killed the tree, I'm not going to die from it."

"Okay," Ronald said, nodding. "So, what were you saying to the tree?"

"It wasn't anything important," Chelsi lied.

Ronald sat down next to her. "Are you thinking about what happened earlier? Are you scared?"

"No. Yes. Maybe. I don't know. Just overwhelmed, is all. And cold."

Ronald put an arm around her shoulders. "It's normal to be scared after something like that. You'll feel better soon. I'm sure we're safe now."

Chelsi nodded. She took a deep breath and tried to calm herself. The wind blew through the trees sending chills up and down her spine, but it helped to clear her head. Then she realized that despite being cold, she was sweating too.

"What's wrong with me?" She asked Ronald.

"Maybe you were so focused on the danger that you didn't notice how hot you became." Ronald suggested. "Or maybe you've been working really hard and haven't noticed until now."

"I guess that does make sense. This has been a rough day."

"Not only today," Ronald said. "But you've had a lot happen in the last week. You should get some sleep."

"That sounds so good right now! And food, definitely some food!"

"Yes! Come on. Let's go back to the house. We can talk more about it when we're warm and dry. I'm worried about you."

"Is this your way of saying you want to stay?" Chelsi asked.

Ronald laughed. "Of course not."

Chelsi laughed as well. "Alright then. Let's go."

***

Little Havana
Abuela's apartment, afternoon

A bright, radiant light shined into Abuela's apartment windows on a beautiful Little Havana afternoon.

Chelsi sat in the kitchen opposite her grandmother, talking about the events in Homestead. Abuela waited patiently, knowing she needed to give her granddaughter time to collect her thoughts. It had been two weeks since Chelsi had faced the Beast, but the scars of that encounter had not fully healed. Chelsi had not told Ronald or Delecruz what had happened to make her find the power to destroy the Beast; she hadn't told anybody. But she felt that she had to tell Abuela because her grandmother had told her that she had felt it all the way here in Little Havana, that incredible surge of power Chelsi had released from the darkness of the void.

Chelsi began to recall the story.

When she finally saw the Beast in real life, her horror had far exceeded what she felt from the nightmares. She would have happily given into despair, but some other emotion took over. Anger. Raw anger more intense and hotter than she had ever felt in her life. She thought about the unfairness of it all, how she would never be able to have a normal life. Chelsi knew she was forever changed. The heat was so intense that she started to feel it manifest in the physical form.

Then she heard the Spirit talk to her.

"You are not alone," it said, "I will help you."

She looked again at the Beast, who stared back with his piercing gaze. Chelsi's anger lessened, and something else came over her instead. A calm confidence that this was no longer just about her anymore. It was bigger than her, bigger than them all. For the first time since the attack, she began to feel hope.

She knew how she would destroy it. Suddenly a light had been switched on. The power from some other world filled her being. She felt that she could do anything, be anything! Her mind raced ahead as if she were running through water, and she was the one controlling the direction of where she went next. A surge of energy coursed through her body, and before long, she was standing tall and powerful. In fact, she seemed larger than life itself.

"¡En tu nombre, ordeno que esta cosa asquerosa muera!"

"In your name, I command this foul thing dead!" she screamed in her mind.

Suddenly there was a flash of light, and Chelsi heard a loud crack! The Beast dropped lifelessly to the ground, its head split open and blood pooling around its body. As soon as the final sound left Chelsi's mouth, her connection to the Spirit was severed. She just stood there, looking down at the massive Beast.

"Chelsi?" someone called in concern.

She barely heard that voice. It was drowned out by other voices, women who, like her, had held the one power in days of the past and who will hold that power in the days of the future!

All this she told her grandmother with tears in her eyes. By the time she finished her story, there were tears in both their eyes.

"Oh mija!" Cried Abuela. "Your mother would be so proud of the woman you have become!"

Chelsi felt a sharp ping of guilt. There was one thing Chelsi didn't tell her grandmother. Something that had been bothering her for the last two weeks.

She was still having nightmares.

***

BOEING DL7382 AIRCRAFT 767-300 to Columbia, 5:30 AM EST.

"This is the captain of Delta flight 89 from Miami," said a calm voice over the intercom. "We are currently inbound into El Dorado International Airport and will be landing shortly. We have been cleared for landing by the tower on Runway 15."

The announcement was followed by an automated weather briefing, which informed passengers that there were scattered clouds at 2,000 feet above ground level with visibility good enough to land all aircraft. The sun would rise at 6:09 a.m., and it would reach its zenith at 10:19 a.m. It was going to be a clear day.

Ronald Stansfield finally relaxed for the first time in five hours as he settled back into his seat after buckling himself up again. He glanced around him and saw that most of the people seated around him had fallen asleep during the final approach. A few minutes later, a soft snoring could be heard from two rows behind him as well.

Knowing the Agency had probably put him on the No-fly list, Ronald had to change his appearance to get through the checkpoints at the Miami international airport. He had shaved off his beard and colored his hair blond. He had stuffed clothes under his shirt to appear to be overweight. He had boarded the plane wearing sunglasses and a baseball cap emblazoned with a logo of a local university. Nobody had even looked twice at him.

He hadn't told his mother or any other of his friends and family where he was going. He knew that they were being watched and their living spaces bugged. He had chosen Columbia since it was a place where you could easily disappear, no one would think to look for him there.

Now here he was, sitting next to a pretty young woman who was dozing off while waiting for the plane to touch down. The captain had announced that they had reached their cruising altitude and asked the passengers to fasten their seatbelts again.

There was no doubt that he should keep his eyes open. They would not not let him out of the airport if they found out who he was. But still . . . he hoped that she didn't notice anything strange about him and just went back to sleep, no disguise held up to very close scrutiny long.

His thoughts were interrupted by the sound of the engines powering down, followed by a soft thump as the wheels hit the runway. A minute later, the pilot's voice came over the intercom system again. "Ladies and Gentlemen, welcome to Bogota, Columbia! Please remain in your seats until we arrive at the gate."

Ronald had a perfect view of the cockpit through the small window in front of them. The pilot was talking to someone on the radio. The flight attendant made an announcement. "This is your captain speaking. I would like to thank you for flying with us today. We hope that you enjoyed your flight. If you have any questions or concerns, please speak to one of our crew members."

The rest of the passengers applauded. Ronald smiled, having just escaped from the clutches of the Agency. He wondered what kind of trouble he would find in Colombia.

"Have you ever been to Colombia before?" asked the girl sitting next to him.

"No," he replied.

She leaned towards him. "I am Maria."

"Justin."

"You sound British. Where are you from, Justin?"

He decided to play along. "I'm from England, actually. Birmingham."

"Never heard of it. So what brings you to Columbia?"

"I saw "Narcos" on Netflix and I thought it's as good a place as any to visit. I'll spend a couple of days in Bogota, then head over to Medellin." He said like he had rehearsed it.

Maria nodded. "Medellin is beautiful. You'll enjoy yourself."

Ronald nodded thankfully. As attractive as she was, he really didn't want the attention right now. He was hoping to go unnoticed.

When the door opened, he got off the plane without anyone looking twice at him. He took care to avoid any eye contact. He would get to his hotel quickly, change clothes and go to a bar to meet some locals, then figure things out from there.

He thought about what went down in Miami. He barely got out of there alive. After the confrontation with the Beast, he was sure that the Agency was onto him and the only way he could stay safe was to make himself scarce. So, he went to a cache in Hialeah were kept a bag with five passports of different countries the Agency would know of so they wouldn't flag, ten thousand American dollars, and five thousand euros and a med kit for the wound he received at the resort. He then went to the closest CVS to get the items for his disguise, and bought a one-way ticket to Bogota.

The whole thing could have gone south fast. He, Chelsi, and Delacruz got extremely lucky. Delacruz walked away with a broken wrist and a concussion. Besides and few bruises, Ronald had escaped virtually unscathed. Physically, Chelsi was fine, but mentally? He could not come close understanding what she was going through, but he thought she would come out of this only stronger.

He was not worried about her. She would pull through. But he was worried about himself. He was a dead man walking now. With the Agency on his trail, he needed to disappear, and fast.

The train arrived at the station in Cali, Colombia. Ronald was carrying his backpack as he exited the station. He was exhausted and jet lagged. After a quick stop at a pharmacy to pick up some painkillers, he went to a café to wait for the bus to take him to the city center.

He ordered a coffee and a croissant. He ate the croissant slowly, enjoying the taste and the feel of the pastry in his hands. He was tired, but he was happy to be back in Columbia, it had been a long time.

He knew he should have felt closure with the victory over that Beast, but something kept nagging at him; the whole thing seemed too . . . neat, too . . . easy. He had plenty of time to think about this. The Beast had been going around Miami for God knows how long, killing and never getting caught. That took a tremendous amount of discretion and planning. An individual that devious would not direct attack, not when it's enemy already saw it coming; this individual would be very methodical.

He remembered when he first faced the Beast at the resort. Ronald thought that the Beast would have to know that there were cameras on the property. How was it so confident that it wouldn't get caught?

Ronald was still trying to figure this out when the bus arrived. He paid the driver, then he boarded and sat down at the back of the bus. The ride to the city center did not take long, maybe twenty minutes. He got off at a main square in the middle of downtown. There were a lot of people milling around, as he walked through the crowded streets, he noticed an increase in police presence.

Finally, he found a hotel near the plaza and checked in. After dropping his bags in room, he went to the lobby to check emails. He had received a message from an unknown sender. It read:

Dear Mr. Stansfield,

I enjoyed out little game together, you turned out to be a very worthy opponent. You may think that you escaped, but you haven't. I can track you anywhere in the world.

Don't worry, I have not told anyone of your location. I prefer to keep that information between us. We can't have you getting arrested now, can we? What would be the fun in that?

Now, I am sure you are wondering how I found out about you. Let's just say I have access to resources similar to the ones available to you during your time at the Agency.

I could have killed you anytime. When you were in Hialeah, for example, but I look forward to playing with you again in the future. Don't go getting yourself killed now, at least not before I get my chance.

Your Friend,
The Beast

A chill ran down his spine as he read it. If this was true, then he was completely screwed. This email was sent from a private account on an encrypted server. There was no way of knowing where it came from or who the sender was. He only knew that it was a threat, and threats were made to be followed through upon.

He quickly shut off his laptop and went into the bathroom to change the bandage on the wound to his forearm. He had been lucky. Knowing what he was dealing with now, he suspected the Beast could have easily cut his arm off if given a chance. As he removed the bandage, he thought about the encounter at the resort. The Beast had had two chances to punch his ticket. Why didn't It just kill him?

He had to admit, he was impressed with himself for surviving. The Beast was like nothing he had ever seen before, and he was certain he would never see another one like it again. As he removed the last bandage, the question that had bothered him was answered.

The wound was fully healed!

Epilogue

Jane Goodman's apartment, evening

Jane Goodman looked at herself in the mirror and made futile attempts to manage her long, unruly, red hair; it had been an exciting month, full of highs and lows.

Dimitri had yet to return her calls. So, she had to assume he was dead. There were more highs, of course, she did feel bad about sacrificing Dimitri. Oh well, she smiled to herself, omelets and eggs! When she had told him about Chelsi Villanueva, he had gotten so angry she had thought that the dullard would ruin her plans! Jane wasn't sure how powerful Chelsi was, so she had needed to toss a sacrificial lamb in Chelsi's path. Despite a few setbacks, she thought the ruse had worked. When she felt Chelsi invade her mind all those weeks ago, she knew the girl was like those Salem witches!! As she thought of them, her anger started to flare. Her eyes began to change and dilate as she looked at herself in the mirror. She let out a sinister laugh that shook the room.

"I'm not some peasant!" she said with her voice deepening, "At least not anymore." Jane then began to recite a verse from one of her favorite scriptures:

"And if ye walk contrary unto me and will not hearken unto me; I will bring seven times more plagues upon you according to your sins."

She began reciting the passage over and over, that her father would quote sometimes as he beat her and her mother! It took her centuries to realize the meaning behind the words, but now they seemed to have taken on a new meaning. She stared into the mirror and saw her face grow distorted; her ears becoming pointed. Red fur started to grow on her forearms. All her beautiful playmates began to spark in her recollection.

She thought it would take all night to get that stupid girl out of the car!

Her hands started elongating, sharp claws began growing out of her enlarged hands. She giggled to herself when she remembered the look of terror on those pups as she dug out that Wynwood girl's spine!!

She began to see the world around her with new clarity, she could smell the thoughts of everyone nearby. The hairs on the back of her neck stood up as she realized that her body was transforming.

In a matter of seconds, Jane Goodman had become something far beyond mortal, or even inhuman.

She thought of how sexy she looked when she went undercover as a lady of the night at the resort to get close to that womanizing fool. She could have killed him cleanly if it wasn't for those damned bodyguards. However, she managed to access the security cameras before killing everybody in the cabana! She regretted not killing the one by the pool; he proved faster than most meat. She might have to tie that loose end up later. Ronald Stansfield, now HE was a worthy adversary! But that night wasn't a total waste!! Thanks to the blood she planted at his residence, everybody thought he was the killer!! The Agency would be relentless now in their pursuit of him!

She felt the power surging through her veins. Her skin grew tight and darkly colored. She opened her mouth wide and felt a snout form. Soon her head had grown larger than any other human skull.

Dimitri Ivanovich, that fool! No style at all! His kills were lazy and clumsy. It was easy to find him by the scent he left behind. She thought how much fun it had been to corner him and give him an offer he couldn't refuse. She would either kill HIM, or make sure he got caught for the assault on the wench downtown, she was an officer of the law after all! So comical! She didn't know which had scared him more!

The rest of her body followed suit, her arms and legs lengthened and became much more muscular. Red fur covered her body, it started to grow thicker and denser as she continued to transform. Once she finished fully transforming, she felt a sense of pride welling up inside her. She had become a beast, a predator, and soon she would be going after her prey.

She realized that this was only the beginning, there was much more to come. She would hunt down the witch, and she would eat her alive and enjoy every minute. Then there would be another, and another until the time came. Then she'd have all of humanity to devour.

Once again, Jane Goodman was ready to take on the world. She would continue to take revenge on society that had abandoned and forsaken her! The revenge she took when finally found her maker centuries later after he forever changed her!

"When every sin has been punished, the Beast is coming for you, Chelsi Villanueva."

Till we meet again. . .playmate!!

***

The End

ABOUT THE AUTHOR

Benjamin J. Burton is the author of *Paradise of Wolf*, his debut paranormal crime thriller. Born in Pittsburgh, Pennsylvania, Benjamin received his Bachelor of Computer Science from Morgan State University. After University, Benjamin enlisted in the US Army, where he served as a paratrooper and at various assignments around the world. Benjamin was awarded numerous medals and commendations during his time in the military, including the Meritorious Service Medal and Bronze Star Medal for Meritorious Service. After leaving the military, he worked for the Department of Defense and the private sector before retiring to become a full-time writer. Benjamin resides in Miami, Florida, where he writes about his favorite subject: murder!